Also by the author:

The Spelling Bee

Raising Kane

Brent Davis

Livingston Press
University of West Alabama

Typesetting and page layout: Angela Brown
Proofreading: Margaret Walburn, Lauren Snoddy,
Mettie Seale, Mary Jo Averette, Angela Brown
Cover design and layout: Angela Brown
Cover photo: Ernie McGuire
Cover Subject: Cody Mcguire, banjo player
visit Cody's website at
codymcguirebanjoplayer.4t.com

This is a work of fiction.
Surely you know the rest: any resemblance
to persons living or dead is coincidental.

Livingston Press is part of The University of West Alabama,
and thereby has non-profit status.
Donations are tax-deductible:
brothers and sisters, we need 'em.
www.livingstonpress.uwa.edu

first edition
6 5 4 3 3 2 1

Raising Kane

To John Hartford

CHAPTER I

My Blue Ridge Cabin Home

BOOM! Rumble!

BOOM! Rumble!

Eddie Kane caught the baseball as it rolled off the roof of his house and then threw it back up.

BOOM! Rumble!

He pretended he was playing second base for the Cardinals. He caught the ball again and imagined throwing it over to Bill White at first base. One away!

Before long his mom would probably stick her head out the door and tell him to quit. Not with company here, she would say. It makes too much racket.

Not that family is really company. But Uncle Berry and Uncle Byron didn't get around too often. They were always on the road.

Eddie studied their car. What was it, anyway? His father called it a "weenie dog car," and it certainly didn't look like the Fords and Chevys Eddie saw in town on Saturdays. He decided it looked like a sedan that had been stretched. Once, he took his Silly Putty and pressed it on a picture of a car he saw in a newspaper ad. Then he pulled the Silly Putty on both ends. It looked like The Bragger Brothers car.

Except it didn't have the bass fiddle strapped to the roof.

If you rode in that car everyone would be looking at you when you came to town.

BOOM! Rumble!

BOOM! Rumble!

Double play!

On some of the baseball teams in Ft. Payne the kids just wore jeans and a t-shirt. But on others you got a full uniform, right down to the stirrup socks. Please, please, now that Mom and Dad are finally going to let me play, please let me be on one of those teams, Eddie said to himself over and over.

"Well, here's what it comes down to." Berry Bragger pushed back his coffee cup, stood at the kitchen table, and began pacing the floor of the small room. "He's old enough to be on the road and you need the money. I'm just saying what needs to be said."

Eddie's mother, Esther, stirred the coffee in her cup and studied the swirling liquid.

"You know we'll watch out for him," Byron continued for his brother. "I know the road's a hard life. I've sat at this very table and complained about how hard it is. But it's better than choppin' cotton."

John Kane sat alone in the overstuffed chair, away from the kitchen table, and winced when he shifted his weight, trying to make himself comfortable.

"A twelve-year old who plays like he does, that's a gift," Byron said quietly.

"And you want to parade him like an organ grinder's monkey in every honky-tonk in the South," Esther said.

"Now, Sister," Berry said, turning to her. "You know we don't play honky-tonks. And we're not going to make a big show out of him. But Byron's right, having him playing with us will be good for business. Folks will hear about it and come see us because of him."

"He hates a fuss being made over him." Esther was no longer talking to her brothers. Instead she was looking at her husband. "Yes, he's musical. But he's shy, too. It's hard for him get up in front of people."

BOOM! Rumble!

"Besides, this is the summer you promised him he could finally play ball. It's all he's talked about."

Byron pursed his lips and waited a moment. Then, he, too, turned to Eddie's father. "I know you've been praying for help since the accident. I know you're worrying about how you're going to pay bills since you can't work. Did you ever stop to think that maybe this is the answer to those prayers?"

Some people say that music lives on Sand Mountain in Alabama like nowhere else. Even today if you visit you'll find people in church playing guitars and mandolins, and when the weather starts getting warm in spring you'll see family bands on front porches playing songs for their neighbors. Drive down a country road and you're likely to see an old gent walking along with a fiddle under his arm. He'll stop in the shade of a big sycamore and play a jig or a reel. Folks say all that music never leaves Sand Mountain. It gets caught in the breezes and swirls through the leaves and it skips along the ground until it's finally leached into the soil. Then there's no getting it out. The music becomes part of the place, just like a tree that comes out of the ground is part of Sand Mountain.

And then the music gets into some of the people on Sand Mountain.

There's always been music in the Bragger side of the family. Eddie's grandpa–his mother's father–was a ginseng man. He collected the root of that plant and sold it all over to folks who believed it cured everything from insomnia to dyspepsia to consumption. But many people said he could heal and bewitch with his fiddle, and that the old tunes he played sweet and low at the end of an all-night barn dance or corn shucking coaxed the old crippled-up farmers and their hobbling wives on to the floor where they danced until morning like bees at the hive.

Byron and Berry began singing before they

could walk. Their mother would take them to the fields and set them in the shade as she began her picking and hoeing and weeding. When they were old enough to tote a sack, the brothers were on their hands and knees in the rows of corn and cotton, hidden from one another by the tall plants. Byron would sing one of the old songs, such as "Barbara Allen" or "The Gypsy Davy," and Berry would answer him in harmony, and they sang all day, every day they were in the fields.

Then they sang their way out of the fields. They were barely teenagers when they won a singing contest at the Spring Valley schoolhouse, where first prize was a gooseberry pie, then at a talent show in Arab they won a five-dollar Sears Roebuck gift certificate, which they traded for a pawn shop guitar. Finally, there was a big show near Bridgeport where a man from a radio station in Tennessee heard them and asked them to sing on his wake-up show at five o'clock every morning.

Their sister, Esther, had music too, but she was the practical one of the bunch and was too busy for singing. She gave her full attention to her sewing and cooking and canning and cleaning and never sang to pass the time or daydreamed about getting off the mountain. She knew the music was powerful and had seen how it had overwhelmed some of the Bragger men. Clarence, a cousin, was good for nothing. He just sat and fiddled, too busy to work while his family went hungry. And Arthur, Junie's boy, was a dandy guitar player. But he went to the city, got in with the wrong crowd, and they never heard from him again. So Esther was scared of music. She knew how it could twist and shape a person's will to suit itself, like how a tree too close to a house will push the foundation out of the way as it grows. She loved music but decided she wouldn't have anything to do with it. When she married John Kane and moved to his farm across the valley, she took her Grandpa's old cigar box banjo to remember the good times, but she never played it.

When Eddie Kane learned to crawl, the first place he went was to the corner where that old banjo was hanging. For weeks he worked at pulling himself up at the wall; then he worked at reaching up and brushing the strings on that old banjo with his fat little fingers. That's when Esther knew he had the music. It had come up in him as naturally as sap rises in a tree that grows on the mountain. She had tried to protect him from the music, to hide him from it. She never let him hear it when he was a baby. She knew how powerful it was. She had seen the way it had taken over Byron and Berry, how it made them worthless for being at home.

But Eddie stood in that corner, reached up, and played "Soldier's Joy" even before he was eating table food. His mother knew there was no sense fighting it—he had music in his bones.

By the time he was three he would sit on the featherbed with the Ring of Fire quilt Granny Bragger had stitched, look out the window at the morning mist burning off the mountain, and pick out the old tunes such as "Arkansas Traveler,"

"Knoxville Girl," and "Devil's Dream." Where had he heard them, Esther wondered. Had those songs been living in the mountain for all these years, waiting for someone to catch them and set them free?

His parents got Eddie a store-bought banjo when he was about five, and he spent many an hour walking Sand Mountain, playing his music. He'd go down the road to the Delmore farm where two or three of the brothers and cousins were always fiddling and carrying on. Old Lady Windell had a player piano at her house in town, which Eddie pumped with his hands because his legs were too short to reach the pedals from the bench. His favorite song was a Sousa march, but the top of the roll was torn and he never learned the name of it.

There was music at concerts and parties and revival meetings, too, and while Eddie loved to listen, he'd never play in front of people. It was all right if there were just a few other musicians around, but he didn't like for people to stare at him and watch his hands as they raced along the neck of his banjo. "Don't be shy, boy! Get on up here!" someone was always yelling at him from the stage at the school auditorium, or from the front of the church. Everyone knew he was a fine musician, but not many people had heard him.

He loved to sit around the wood stove on the front porch and play with Byron and Berry when they came for a visit. They had a radio show of their own by then and drove all over the country in their big car playing state fairs, festivals, and at Moose lodges and Mason halls. They invited Eddie to be on the radio with them, but he declined. "I couldn't do that," he stammered. Just the thought of standing on stage terrified him, let alone picking tunes with people watching. He was happy to stay at home and wander the mountain making his music.

If he got his music from his mother's side of the family, he must have gotten his love for baseball from his father. John Kane was one of the best pitchers ever on Sand Mountain and had a tryout with a farm league team for the St. Louis Browns when he got out of high school. World War II interrupted his plans, though, and after he spent a couple of winters in the mud and snow in Italy, his arthritis got so bad he could hardly run the base paths. The old timers in town still called him "Candy" Kane, which was the nickname he earned for his sweet swing and peppermint red hair, an attribute Eddie shared with his father. "I'll never forget that game against Hartselle," some old timer would tell Eddie when he stopped at the store in town for some hoop cheese and soda crackers. "Candy Kane hit four home runs that day and fanned the order two times!"

John Kane's legs were so weak that he had been using a cane ever since Eddie could remember. Still, he insisted on doing as much work as he could on the farm and did more work than able-bodied men twice his size.

Eddie had chores on the farm, too. Every morning he gathered eggs from the henhouse and filled the wood box by the stove in the kitchen.

His dad milked the few cows that he kept on the place–mostly they were raising turkeys in a big, long house that had been built with money borrowed from the processing plant–but it was Eddie's job to put out hay for the bull. There was only one bull on the place, but he was cantankerous and ornery and Eddie hated being around him.

One day Eddie was at the Delmore place learning a new song called "Billy in the Low Ground." It was getting late and he knew he should be getting back home to finish his chores. But his father never begrudged him his music time, and he'd finish up Eddie's work.

It was dark by the time Eddie had mastered the new tune and finally started home. There was an eerie silence when he entered the house and no one answered when he called. Supper was still on the stove, but it hadn't been served and was getting cold. Perplexed, Eddie called the Coopers, the family on the next farm up the road.

"Did you do your chores today, boy?" Mrs. Cooper said slowly.

"Yes, ma'am."

"Don't you lie to me, boy! I know better! There's never been a dishonest Kane on this mountain. Don't you be the first!" She paused and then lowered her voice. "Your daddy's been hurt. That old bull gored him. Now, what in the world John Kane with his legs like they are was doing in a pen with that bull, I'll never know."

Eddie Kane cried all night long. It's my

fault that my daddy was hurt because he was doing my chores, he kept sobbing. Mrs. Cooper had told him that his parents would be gone all night and that he should come over to her house if he was scared or got lonely. It was the first night he spent alone. He was eleven years old, but that night he cried like a baby.

John Kane had been gored in the right hip, and now it was a struggle for him to cross the room, let alone do the work around the farm. His bachelor brother Milton moved in to help, but there was more for Eddie to do, too.

That summer they got their first television. Some of the folks in town took up a collection when they heard about John's accident and decided that since he couldn't get out as easily, he might like to watch baseball games on TV. Every Saturday afternoon Eddie would join his father on the divan and they'd watch the Game of the Week, brought to you by Lectra Shave.

Eddie's favorite player was an outfielder named Willie Mays. One time they were watching a tie game in the ninth inning when a ball was hit way to his right.

Eddie spanked his hands together. "That's the ball game. He'll never get it."

"You just watch," said his dad.

Mays didn't even look like he was running fast, but he covered more ground than a tarpaulin and made an over-the-shoulder basket catch.

"Did you see that?" Eddie said, jumping up from the couch and pumping his arms in the air.

His dad smiled and nodded. "He's maybe the

greatest outfielder I ever saw. But I have to admit, it's still a little funny for me to see a colored fellow playing in the big leagues."

Eddie looked at his father quizzically.

"Wasn't too long ago that coloreds couldn't play with everyone else."

"How come?"

"That's just the way it was. Especially in the South. Not so much here on the mountain. Never was many colored folks up here. The farms was too small, too rocky. Couldn't have big plantations to grow cotton like in the rest of the state where they bought up slaves to work in the fields."

"Did you play against colored men?"

His father shook his head, then shifted his leg, which was propped up in a chair, and winced. "No. But I saw a lot of them play in the Negro leagues. Some of them was real good."

"I'm glad I get to see Willie Mays on TV."

"He's an Alabama boy."

"Really?"

"He grew up in Birmingham. But if he was there now, he wouldn't be playing with the whites. That's for sure. Things may have changed, but they haven't changed that much."

"Dad, does it ever make you mad that you aren't playing?" Eddie asked, nodding toward the Zenith.

"Used to make me mad every time I was staring at the backside of a mule, plowing. But. . ." His voice trailed away and he turned and looked out the window. "When I was your age I couldn't wait to get off this mountain. But now I'm glad

I'm back. This is where I belong."

The picture was fading. Eddie had gotten up and adjusted the rabbit ear antenna until the stadium came into sharper view. Somehow it made him feel better knowing that Willie Mays, an Alabama boy, could do what he did in front of all those people.

BOOM! Rumble!
BOOM! Rumble!

Eddie loved living on the mountain, but he hated doing the chores on the farm. He knew it was his fault his dad had been hurt, and he knew they needed help to keep the farm going. He also knew he was a good musician and he sensed it was time to do something with his music. Sand Mountain hadn't given up all of its songs to him just so he could keep them to himself. Maybe it was time that he shared what he knew.

He threw the ball straight up in the air and practiced his pop flies. He tried an over-the-shoulder basket catch but missed, and the ball rolled away from him. He made a fist and jammed it into his baseball glove. I've got a lot to learn, he thought.

He knew why his uncles were visiting. They wanted him in their band. But it would mean being away from home and getting up to play in front of all those people. And it would mean he might never get to play in the Sand Mountain baseball league.

But it was the only way he could think of to get out of doing the chores. He could send the money his uncles gave him back to his father to help keep the farm going.

Eddie Kane ran around the house because he thought if he walked he might get to thinking about it again and lose his nerve. He stuck his head in the door, interrupting Uncle Byron. "Okay. I'll go," he announced.

CHAPTER II

Hard, Ain't It Hard

"Red-Haired Boy."

"Again?" Eddie asked his Uncle Berry.

"Again."

Eddie started the song for what seemed like the hundredth time, the fingers on his right hand snapping and rolling on the banjo strings. With his left hand he moved up and down the instrument's neck, almost like he was tickling a tune out of the thing. It was cramped and uncomfortable playing in the car, but this was the only chance to rehearse. They were on their way to an early morning radio show in Bristol, Tennessee, then they'd be off to play somewhere else that night.

Berry crisply chopped the rhythm of the song, playing his mandolin on the backbeat. They'd been working on this tune ever since they drove off Sand Mountain, and time and again Berry

Brent Davis

kept getting after Eddie. "You're speeding up. It's not a race."

What time is it? Eddie wondered. Seems like it's been dark forever. They had stopped only once at a tiny diner Byron called a "hash house" and everyone ate barbecue because it was the only thing on the menu. Except the fiddle player, whose name Eddie didn't quite catch. He ate fries and white bread and a couple of slices of pie.

Eddie thought the fiddle player was asleep. His eyes were closed and his head was slumped over, but at the end of the first verse he joined the tune again. Only he wasn't using a bow. He was playing the violin like a guitar and picking out the notes. It finally dawned on Eddie that you couldn't bow a fiddle in the car—you'd keep hitting the roof or poke out someone's eye. The fiddle was soft and quiet when it was picked. Eddie liked it.

The man driving the car was named Cecil. He was the comedian of the group, though Eddie thought his jokes were pretty corny every time he'd seen his uncles play. While the rest of the band wore a white shirt and black tie, Cecil dressed like a hillbilly and wore overalls that were cut off at the knee. He also blacked out a couple of his teeth, wore a tattered hat, and talked like a hick. Cecil played the big bass fiddle that was strapped to the top of the car.

Byron was in the front seat, too, his eyes closed and his chin on his chest. Eddie thought he was asleep, but he was working the car radio all the time. He kept it low so it wouldn't

interrupt the rehearsal in the back seat, but
he was constantly turning the dial, going from
one country station to the next. He hated rock-
n-roll. Every time he came across a rock-n-
roll station he would shake his head and mutter
something about Elvis Presley. "He's killing
our music," he said. "All the stations that
were playing our kind of music have switched to
hootchy kootchy bands playing electric guitars
and drums."

And the news seemed to agitate Cecil. Every
hour, on the hour, every station would feature
an announcer giving the headlines. "I'll be
switched!" Cecil said after hearing about plans
to launch a second Mercury astronaut into space.
"They're not fooling me! That's just make-
believe, like in a movie!" And he shook his head
after a story about Freedom Riders–people who
were challenging the practice in the South that
made Negroes sit in the back of the bus and use
separate waiting rooms. "Those Freedom Riders
better not be on this highway. I'll show them a
little Southern hospitality!"

They kept practicing "Red-Haired Boy" forever,
it seemed to Eddie, then Berry had him play
along on the band's theme song, a twenty-second
little ditty extolling the virtues of Excelsior
Corn Starch, the sponsor of The Bragger Brothers
Weekly Wake-Up Radio Show. "It's in the bright
red package at your local grocery store," Berry
sang, and then the rest of the band responded,
"Make a greater gravy, with Ex-cel-si-or!" Berry
made Eddie sing, too, though singing wasn't
exactly Eddie's strong suit.

Finally Berry said they'd practiced enough and put his mandolin back in its case. Eddie's banjo was too big to take off and put up without bumping into the fiddle player and Uncle Berry, so he just kept it on. His fingers ached from playing so long and his back was sore from holding his heavy banjo and sitting funny in the car.

As tired as he was, though, he couldn't help but pull the piece of paper from his shirt pocket, unfold it, and study it whenever enough light spilled into the car. It was the set list Uncle Byron had given him, and it thrilled Eddie to know he was going to be playing these songs with one of the best bands anywhere. He mouthed the titles of the songs, especially pleased with the silent rhythm formed by the words of the oldest tunes:

My Blue Ridge Cabin Home
Hard, Ain't It Hard
Gotta Travel On
Leather Britches
Paddy on the Turnpike
Fiddler's Dream
Devil's Dream
Good Times Are Past and Gone
Soldier's Joy
'Tis Sweet To Be Remembered
River of Jordan
Don't Let Your Deal Go Down
Dixie Breakdown
We Live in Two Different Worlds
Heavy Traffic Ahead
Red-Haired Boy
Bright Morning Stars

Eddie pursed his lips. He was familiar with the songs, but most would take as much work as "Red-Haired Boy" to really master.

In the front seat Eddie could see that Byron's head was resting on his shoulder, and soon Berry began snoring. The fiddle player's head was tilted back against the cushion, his mouth hanging open. What time is it? Eddie wondered. Long after midnight, he guessed. Everyone's asleep but Cecil and me, Eddie thought. And I'm not sure about him. Cecil sat without moving, his eyes squinched so tightly he might have nodded off, too.

Eddie thought about the big feather bed he slept on at home. This early in the summer up on the mountain if you slept with the window open, as Eddie did, you'd still need a quilt. The breeze would gently stir the curtains and you could hear the trees sway and dance.

And what did Mom fix for supper? he wondered. Fried chicken with mashed potatoes? With creamed corn she'd put up from the garden last year? His mouth watered. The thin, dry sandwich he'd had at the hash house that night had disappeared in about four or five bites. He wished he had something to eat right now.

He closed his eyes and tried to sleep, but nothing happened. He wiggled and then folded his hands behind his head, trying to make a pillow, but he couldn't get comfortable. Finally he sighed, gave up, and stared at the dark shapes outside the window in the moonless landscape.

"Hey, Kid."

Eddie turned to his left and found the fiddle

player looking at him.

"Get a load of this." The fiddler stuck out his hand, offering him something.

"Listen," he insisted.

Eddie reached into the man's open palm and found he was holding an earplug. The man pulled back his jacket and revealed a transistor radio in his shirt pocket. He smiled.

Eddie put the earpiece in his ear and heard the howling guitars of rock and roll music.

"It's Elvis doing 'Rock a Hula Baby' on Murray the K's show," the fiddle player whispered.

Eddie listened for a bit. He had a radio by his bed back home, but mostly he listened to baseball games at night. Back on Sand Mountain, lots of folks said rock and roll music wasn't music at all. At one of the churches, he'd heard them say it was the work of the devil.

"Murray the K's show is out of New York. 'Murray the K and the Swingin' Soiree.' Your uncles don't care for it too much."

Eddie nodded and listened some more. He hadn't heard anything like "Rock a Hula Baby" on Sand Mountain.

"You like him?"

Eddie shrugged. Murray the K was certainly energetic. He could talk a mile a minute.

"I think he's boss."

Do what? Eddie wondered. The fiddle player seemed to be an unlikely rock and roll fan. He was probably about twenty, Eddie guessed, and was tall and skinny with a head full of thick hair. The way he played, Eddie figured he must have been raised on Sand Mountain, too.

The fiddle player stuck out his hand. At first Eddie thought he wanted his earplug back, but then he realized he was being offered a handshake. "I'm Murray Singer. Murray—just like Murray the K."

"Eddie Kane. Just like the candy cane."

Murray smiled. He took the earplug from Eddie. "I like to listen because it reminds me of home. His radio studio is just a few blocks from where my parents live."

Eddie folded his arms. He couldn't believe it. "You're from New York?"

Murray nodded.

"How'd you learn to play the fiddle like that?"

Murray shrugged. "You can find old-time music up there if you look hard enough. And there's lots of folk musicians like Pete Seeger. You ever heard of him?"

Eddie shook his head.

"And one of my uncles played fiddle in a Klezmer band."

"A what band?"

"I'll play some for you sometime."

Eddie rested his eyes for a minute and listened to the hum of the car tires on the pavement. Every picture he'd seen of New York at night showed the skyscrapers all lit up. Do the people there ever sleep when it's dark? he wondered. Then he finally fell asleep.

Brent Davis

CHAPTER III

Gotta Travel On

"Up and at 'em, Boy!"

Eddie felt an elbow in his ribs and blinked his eyes open. He was still in the back of the car, and it was still dark, but they had stopped and the others were piling out.

"We got no time to lose!" Uncle Berry continued, reaching for his mandolin.

Eddie slid across the backseat, his banjo still around his neck, swung his feet out of the car, and stood up. His left leg was asleep, and he staggered as he followed the others into a small cinderblock building. He figured he must have tossed and turned in the car because his shirt was nearly twisted backward at his waist. He tried to straighten it as he walked.

"I was beginning to wonder if you boys was going to make it this time," Eddie heard a voice crackle from a speaker on the wall. He surveyed the room but there was no one there. Then he looked through a window about the size of a school flag and saw a man in an adjoining room behind a console wearing a headset. Eddie's eyes were still adjusting to the light, but he could make out metal cabinets of tubes, wires, and dials. This is a radio station, he realized. A huge clock on the wall read 4:59.

The Bragger Brothers busied themselves getting their instruments strapped on and tuned up. Murray turned away from the others, his fiddle under his chin, and practiced a lick. A moment later Cecil entered the room carrying the big bass fiddle that had been strapped to the roof of the car.

"Oh, my lumbago!" he protested loudly.

"It's five a.m. and you're listening to WLBD, the musical voice of Dixie, from Bristol, Tennessee." Eddie looked around and saw the man with the headsets was talking again. Bristol, he thought. Nice of the man to tell him where he was.

"Bet you a silver dollar–it's music from the hills and hollers! Here they are, for your early morning, wake-up pleasure, all the way from high atop Sand Mountain, The Bragger Brothers!"

Oh. It's a radio show, Eddie thought, smiling because he finally figured out what was going on. Then Uncle Berry grabbed him by the sleeve and jerked him into the circle the others had formed around a big microphone on a silver stand. With a lightning-quick run on the bass strings of his guitar, Byron kicked off the theme song

Eddie had learned in the car just a few hours ago. Eddie automatically joined in. "It's in the bright red package at your local grocery store," Berry sang, and then they all chimed in, "Make a greater gravy–with Excel-si-or!"

"Good morning and thank you for joining us," Byron said, the "Excelsior Corn Starch Theme Song" still ringing in the studio. "We're The Bragger Brothers from Sand Mountain, Alabama, and it's an honor and a privilege to be with you this morning. We're going to continue with a number that features the newest member of the group, a fellow who's a whiz on the banjo and just happens to be the youngest member of our group–or any group, I reckon–twelve year-old Eddie Kane, who's going to show us how to do a little 'Shuckin' the Corn!'"

Eddie's fingers were flying along the frets even before his uncle's mouth was shut. He ripped through the verse and the chorus and was playing a little back-up while Murray fiddled the lead before he started thinking about what he was doing. I'm playing on the radio, he thought. Even people all the way back on Sand Mountain might be listening on WLBD. There's thousands and thousands of people all over listening to me right now.

Then his mind went mostly blank. It seemed like the only thing that existed was the song, and he wasn't aware of anything else until the song was over. He knew he got the ending right– his "shave and a haircut, two bits" lick was still echoing in his ears. But what about the rest? Had he even been playing during the last half of the song?

"All right, all right." Now it was Berry at the microphone. "Whoa! That is some fine picking! And this early in the morning! That was Eddie Kane, the twelve-year-old terror of the banjo from Sand Mountain, Alabama!"

Eddie looked around the room. The man with the headset was sitting back in his chair with his arms folded behind his head. His uncles were looking at each other as they told the listeners about the rich, thick gravy you could make with Excelsior Cornstarch. Cecil was yawning, his head leaning against the bass fiddle. Murray was resting the fiddle in the crook of his arm. Then he winked at Eddie.

I guess I did all right, Eddie thought. I didn't faint or fall over during the song. I didn't forget how to play it or have to start over like little kids do in piano recitals I've seen. Shoot. There's nothing special about playing on the radio. You're just in a room with the guys who you've been playing with for so long anyway. There's no one to see you, to look at you.

Like when you're on stage, in person.

The radio show was only fifteen minutes long. Byron and Berry did a song alone, and then they did "Leaning On the Everlasting Arms" like a gospel quartet. Byron was the only one playing on that, but Cecil, Murray, and Byron sang harmony. There were more commercials, Cecil told a corny joke in his hick accent, Byron read a letter from a fan–though Eddie noticed there was no paper in his hands, so he wondered if his uncle was making it up—and then they did "Cripple Creek," a song Eddie could play in his sleep. Berry talked about some of the places The Bragger Brothers would be appearing—there was a drive-in and a fish fry and a school concert mentioned—and then the man with the headsets signaled them to "wrap it up."

"That's all the time we've got for this edition of the Early Morning Weekly Wake-Up Radio Show," Byron said, "so we're going to head down the highway, through the hills and hollers, and we'll look for you where the road rises and the skies are blue." They raced through the theme song one more time and then they were back outside, loading up the car.

They stopped to eat at a truck stop outside of Bristol. Eddie followed the others as they snaked their way past diesel trucks, their engines idling. The ground seemed to rumble and throb. Eddie had never seen so many trucks in one place. What was the loudest, longest noise he'd heard on Sand Mountain? A tractor? A rooster at daybreak?

"Well, Kid, you did all right," Murray told him as they opened their menus. Eddie's uncles and Cecil were sitting at their own table. It reminded Eddie of holiday meals at his granddaddy's house and how the kids always got put at their own table.

Murray held out his coffee cup so the passing waitress would be sure to notice it, and then continued. "It won't suit your uncles—you sped up a bit on your solo—but you did just fine."

Eddie's face was buried in the menu, but suddenly he got that nervous feeling in his stomach again. He realized he probably wasn't good enough to be playing with his famous uncles.

"Your uncles are hard to please," Murray said. "They've been doing this for thirty years and they don't have much to show for it except an old, beat-up car. The music is all that's really theirs. So they're proud of it. They want it to be just right."

Murray turned his menu over and ran his finger down the page. "My fiddle playing doesn't suit them, either."

"But you're the best fiddler I've ever heard!" Eddie insisted. "How can they be disappointed with your playing?"

"I'm not perfect. That's what they're looking for."

"Well, I'm not perfect neither. And I never will be."

"No, we won't. But here's how to tell you're getting close." Murray picked up a package of saltines, opened it, and popped both in his mouth. "When you stop thinking about the music and just feel the music taking over, that's where you want to be."

CHAPTER IV

Leather Britches

After breakfast they were back in the car and speeding down the highway. Byron drove and Cecil slept in the front seat. Berry, Eddie, and Murray worked up a new song in the back. Eddie knew "Up and Far Away," a tune the Bragger Brothers had played for years and years, but he'd never done it with them.

"Start your solo up here high on the neck," Byron said, pointing at Eddie's banjo. "Make it choppy–not smooth–on this song. And don't speed up. You sped up this morning."

Murray couldn't hide a smile as he plucked his fiddle.

"What's so funny?" Byron asked "You slowed down on your break." He turned back to Eddie. "Try it again."

They kept playing "Up and Far Way" as the

car made its way along a winding river and then climbed the mountains. They practiced through towns so small Berry didn't bother slowing as he whisked through them and they practiced through bigger towns with traffic lights and grocery stores and farm tractor dealerships. Eddie didn't know where they were going, but he heard Byron say they were supposed to be there by two.

He looked at his wristwatch. That was less than an hour away. He'd have to stand up in front of a bunch of people and play then.

Eddie had almost fallen into a trance, playing the same song over and over, but he was awakened by the flash of lightning and the crack of thunder. Rain pelted the car and Berry turned on the windshield wipers. But he didn't slow down. I'm glad I'm not driving, Eddie thought, peering out the window. You can't see a thing.

"I'm telling you, Brother, I just got a feeling about this summer," Berry said, leaning forward over the steering wheel and peering through the front windshield.

Byron didn't respond. He sat with his arms folded, chewing on the side of his cheek. He looked out the window and scanned the sky, looking for a break in the clouds.

"Something's going to go our way this summer, you just watch," Berry continued. "It's bound to, finally."

Eddie had listened to enough conversations at the dinner table to know that his father considered Berry the talker of the two brothers. Especially when he was nervous. The car dipped off the shoulder for a moment, kicked up gravel and mud that clattered in the wheel well, and then Berry pulled the vehicle back on to the pavement.

"Look at Monroe. He's getting his big tent show together again this summer. You've heard everyone talk about it. Someone's bound to notice us—maybe we can talk Bill into letting us get in on that. Then we'll have it made."

A show with Bill Monroe? Eddie sat up straighter. Monroe was the best musician he knew of. He was everyone's favorite. Eddie's hands turned clammy just thinking about sharing a stage with Bill Monroe.

"Know what I remember from the first time I saw Bill Monroe?" Cecil asked.

Berry shrugged. "What?"

"A baseball game. Back then when he come to town everyone in his band would be on a team and they'd play the team from that local town. Everybody turned out to see if their local boys could whup Mr. Monroe's team."

Byron nodded. "That's right. You didn't have to be a great fiddler or a banjo picker to get a job with Bill back then, but you sure had to be able to hit a curveball."

It was just a couple of minutes before two when Berry turned into a car lot in a little town. Eddie thought maybe he was asking for directions, but then he saw a small, open-sided tent with red and white balloons tied to the poles. The balloons were thrashing in the wind and rain. "Studebaker Summer Clearance Sale Spectacular!" Eddie saw painted on the windows of the showroom. "Live Entertainment!"

Berry pulled up as close to the tent as he could and everyone grabbed their instruments.

"Is this it?" Eddie asked Murray.

Murray looked around and shrugged. He reached behind the back seat for the four hats that had been stored there and distributed them to the members of the band. Then he pulled his shirt out of his pants, stuck his fiddle up under it, and dashed to the tent. Eddie followed him, hugging his banjo to his chest to protect it from the rain.

Byron, Murray, and Eddie huddled under the tent while Cecil and Berry struggled in the rain to get the bass off the roof of the car. The three of them tuned up and stamped their feet to get the circulation going. And to warm up a bit. Even though it's May, that's a cold rain, Eddie thought.

Berry and Cecil hurried in out of the rain, and Cecil untied the tarpaulin that was wrapped around his bass. "Red-Haired Boy," Byron said, still tuning his guitar.

"But there's no one here," Eddie said.

"They'll come."

So Eddie kicked off the song. The wind blew, the rain fell harder, and Eddie saw two men inside the showroom watching them. This is crazy, he thought. The wind was blowing the rain up under the tent and Eddie pressed up against Murray, trying to stay dry.

They went through a dozen numbers. All the ones they had worked up in the car and old tunes Eddie had been playing since he first started on the banjo.

The rain never let up, but eventually one car pulled up alongside the tent and the driver rolled down his window. There's a whole family in there, Eddie realized, looking through the raindrops on the glass. The way they're crowded up, there might be two or three families in that car.

Then another car drove up, and another. The passengers never got out, and Eddie couldn't see them. But they were listening to the music. When they finished "The Banks of the Ohio," Eddie could hear muffled applause.

"I told you they'd come," Byron said softly, turning to Eddie.

Byron and Berry tore off on an instrumental duet version of "Redwing." Even though the rain was pouring down and there were only a handful of people listening, Eddie couldn't remember his uncles ever playing with more energy and excitement.

They kept playing and playing. The damp weather made it hard for Eddie to keep his banjo in tune, and he was cold and miserable. Cecil did his hillbilly comedy routine but there wasn't anyone around to laugh at the jokes.

For his first bit, Cecil carried his bass in front of the rest of them and pleaded with Berry for the chance to sing a solo.

"Maybe you should sing it so low we can't hear you," Berry answered, as he always did, but there was no laughter.

But Cecil won the argument and he introduced his heartache song by taking off his worn hobo's hat and wringing it in his hands.

Then he started singing. And it was terrible. His voice cracked and slipped and slid around the notes. But after just a couple of lines the song was interrupted by something ringing. Without pausing, Cecil opened a small door on the back of his bass fiddle, pulled out a clanging alarm clock, and turned it off.

"Wait a minute, wait a minute!" Berry said, stopping the song. "Cecil, what on earth are you doing with an alarm clock?"

"Well, when you hired me you said you wanted me to play bass to help the band keep time." He looked at the clock. "It's five-fifteen!"

Then Murray played a little "shave and a haircut, two bits" line on his fiddle to announce the end of the comedy routine. "Cecil, next time you want to sing a solo, stand next to a window and I'll help you out," Berry said, delivering a line that usually got a pretty good laugh. As the band regrouped Murray turned his back to everyone but Eddie. "What kind of idiot cuts a hole in the back of a bass violin?" he said out of the side of his mouth.

They played for about an hour, then ran to the car and sat shivering in wet clothes while Berry argued with a man inside the showroom.

Cecil, who had gotten thoroughly drenched strapping his bass to the roof of the car, drove to the showroom door. Finally Berry slowly walked out and got in.

"How much did you get?" Byron asked as Cecil sped away.

"I got all of it."

Murray found a dry towel on the floor and handed it to Cecil, who took off his hat and passed it back. Byron and Berry handed their hats back, too, and Murray placed them next to his side-by-side on the shelf behind the back seat.

"What'd he say?" Byron asked.

"Said we didn't pull in a crowd and he didn't sell any cars and he wasn't going to pay us. I said it wasn't our fault it turned up a frog strangler and he still owed us what he said he was going to give us."

Berry paused and fished a comb out of his back pocket. He swept his jet-black hair straight back.

"Then I said, 'Mister, sounds like you want to play hardball. You ever been to Sand Mountain?' And he says, no he never has been there. And I say, 'Well, sir, it's a beautiful place, and you owe it to yourself to see that part of the country.' Then I say 'There's two things we love on Sand Mountain. First is music. The second thing is baseball.' Then I tell him how much we miss playing baseball because we're driving all over creation doing these shows. But you'd be surprised, I tell him, because even though we're out of practice we're still pretty handy with a bat. Then I say, 'If you don't give me our money by the count of three, I'm going to go to that car, tell the boys to get their bats, and we're going to break every window on every car you've got. Then we're going to break every window in the showroom.' Berry stopped. Then I told him we'd come looking for him."

Berry put his hands behind his head and stretched out his legs. "So he gets all red in the face and puffs up and says just try it, he's got a garage full of big, mean mechanics. Then I says, 'Well, bring 'em on, cause we've been holed up in that car and we're ready for some exercise.'"

Eddie was mortified. He didn't want to get in a fight with anybody! He was just a kid who played the banjo! "Then what happened?"

"Then he gave me the money and he ran like a scalded dog!"

Cecil laughed, Byron smiled, and Murray just shook his head. As they celebrated, Berry pulled a roll of bills from his pocket and began handing them out. "Welcome to the wonderful world of professional music," he said, giving Eddie one dollar. "I'm sending the rest back to your daddy."

CHAPTER V

Paddy On The Turnpike

That afternoon they practiced more songs as they hurtled down the highway. Eddie didn't ask where they were headed. He didn't want to think about how many people he might be playing in front of when they got there. Around dusk they pulled into a little town and he saw a sign stretched over the street that read "Montgomery County Volunteer Fire Department Fish Fry."

They parked the car and Murray reached behind him and distributed the hats. They got out and stood for a minute in the fading sun.

"Feels good after wading through that mess this afternoon," Byron said.

"Hmm," Berry agreed.

Someone ushered them to the head of a line that was forming at the food table.

"That'll be a dollar-fifty," said a woman

sitting behind a table. She stuck her hand out to Eddie.

Murray tipped his hat to her. "He's with the band, Ma'am."

"I couldn't tell. He doesn't have a hat."

"Well, we don't give a hat to just anybody in this outfit."

The food was delicious. Eddie ate so much of the golden brown, crispy pieces of fish that it seemed as if his banjo stuck out a couple of inches farther when it hung in front of his stomach. He washed it all down with sweet tea and stuffed himself with hush puppies and homemade ice cream when there wasn't any fish within reach.

"Where you from, Son?" asked one of the men as he pulled the wire basket full of fish out of the boiling oil.

"Up on Sand Mountain, in Alabama, sir."

"Don't they have fish up there?"

"Yes, sir, we've got fish."

The man laughed. "Well, you're eating like you've never had any before."

Once they began playing it didn't occur to Eddie to be nervous. After all, it was just a party. Everyone was walking around with paper plates full of food and talking and laughing. He'd been to dozens of barbecues and cookouts back home. This was no different. He wasn't even thinking of the crowd. After Byron told the people that because everyone had just celebrated Mother's Day they were going to do "Wildwood Flower" by Mother Maybelle Carter, Eddie couldn't help but think about his mother.

Last year he had given her a Mother's Day card he had made out of red construction paper, but he didn't think to make her anything before he hit the road with his uncles. It seemed like forever since he had seen her.

Then Berry introduced him as "The Twelve-Year-Old Terror of the Five-String Banjo" and had him take three solos on "Gold Rush," the instrumental they'd worked up in the car that afternoon.

Someone in the crowd whooped. "Play it, Boy!" a man yelled. It startled Eddie and made him suddenly realize that everyone was watching him. He faltered for just an instant, missed several notes, and had to scramble to catch up with the others.

Or maybe his hands were just greasy from the fish.

That night in the car Byron was driving. He suddenly snapped off the radio. "Boys, we've got a problem," he declared.

Uh-oh, Eddie thought. This is where he really lets me have it for messing up that song this evening. I ruined everything when I flubbed that instrumental. Maybe they were going to kick him out of the band.

Byron put on the turn indicator and Eddie saw they were pulling into a truck stop. He caught a flash in the car's headlights of a gray metal sign shaped like a sprinting dog. It's a Greyhound bus stop! They're going to throw me out of the band and put me on the next bus home!

"She's running hot," Byron said. "Let's give her a look."

"I remember the old boy who has this place," Cecil said. "He's a dandy mechanic."

The band trooped into the truck stop carrying shaving kits and travel bags to freshen up while Byron and the mechanic looked at the car. Eddie had his extra clothes in a paper sack, and when he set it down on the floor of the men's room it fell over. A baseball rolled out of it. Eddie grabbed it and stuffed it back in the sack. Don't know why I put my ball and glove in there, he thought. It's just taking up space.

After getting into a clean pair of pants, he hurried into the dining room, dug the dollar out of his pocket, and asked for change at the counter. The man there nodded, and as he fished the coins out of the cash register, Eddie read a sign that had been taped to the front of it. "Attention Interstate Travelers!" it read. "The bus company is not responsible for . . ."

The man at the counter interrupted him and counted out the coins as they clinked in Eddie's open palm. ". . . fifty, seventy-five, one dollar," he said, and then he used his belly to push the cash register drawer closed. "That business has a lot of our drivers pretty upset," the man said, nodding at the notice that Eddie was reading.

"What's it about?"

"The integrationists. They're really stirring things up."

A bell rang behind him. "Order up!" called a voice from the kitchen, and the man left to serve the food.

Eddie couldn't figure out who was stirring things up for the bus company, and he didn't really care. He knew he didn't have much time. So he hurried into a phone booth, closed the door behind him, and dialed the operator.

"May I help you?" said a thin voice.

"Yes, Ma'am. I want to call my momma up on Sand Mountain in Alabama."

The operator asked for the number then told him to deposit fifty-five cents for the first three minutes. Eddie tried to explain that he only had quarters and couldn't put in the exact amount.

"Fifty-five cents, please," the woman said more urgently.

"Just a minute." Maybe he had a nickel in his pocket. No, not in the left one. Maybe the right.

"That will be fifty-five cents."

"Ma'am, I don't have fifty-five cents and I'm not sure I gave you the right number when you asked me where I was calling."

"I'll check the listing," the woman said. "What's the name?"

"Esther. My mom's name is Esther Kane."

"One moment, please." Then, after a brief silence, the woman continued. "I'm sorry, but I have no listing for Esther Kane. Or for Sand Mountain. Please tell me the town or city of this residence."

"Sand Mountain's not really the town," he said, still looking for a nickel. "The school's in Geraldine, but the post office is in Albertville. We're kind of between them. I'm not sure which one the phone company says is our home. We just always tell people we live on Sand Mountain."

"I have no Esther Kane listed for Geraldine. Please spell the name of the other town."

"A-l-b-e-r..."

Eddie was interrupted by knocking on the telephone booth. He looked through the window and saw Cecil waving at him to follow. "Come on! We got to get moving!" Cecil called.

"I've got to go," Eddie told the operator. He hung up, raked the coins off the shelf under the phone where he had counted them out, grabbed his sack of clothes, and ran to the car. They were rolling even before he slammed the door.

Byron sniffed and rolled his neck, ready for the next leg of the trip, and everyone settled in their seats. "Just a busted radiator hose," he said.

"Told you he was a good mechanic," Cecil said.

Byron nodded. "We're running cooler, but we're behind schedule."

For the next couple of hours they practiced an instrumental called "Back Up and Push." They just kept playing it over. And over. And over. No one said anything until Murray played an unusual lick on the fiddle. Eddie liked it—it sounded vaguely familiar—but when Cecil heard it his head snapped. "That ain't mountain music!" he spat. He turned to Berry. "That's an electric guitar lick he stole off the radio! He listens to that rock and roll at night, when he thinks the rest of us are asleep!" He turned back to Murray. "We got to keep our music pure. We don't need your kind and your crazy music!"

Murray looked down at his fiddle, pretending to be preoccupied with something on the fingerboard. He scratched it gently with a fingernail. He didn't look up until Cecil had turned around. Then he glanced out the window, chewed his lower lip for a moment, and then kicked off "Back Up and Push" once again.

Berry joined in, and Eddie did, too, but his fingers were killing him. His back hurt from holding the banjo. And he was dead tired. But when they finally quit practicing he couldn't get to sleep. He couldn't help thinking of home. It seemed like ages since he had talked to his mother and father.

CHAPTER VI

Fiddler's Dream

Eddie was still awake when they pulled over to swap drivers. What day of the week is it? he wondered. He closed his eyes and tried counting sheep. He had heard that worked when you were tired, but still, he was restless. He could hear the whine of the tires on the pavement and snoring and whistling noises as Byron, Berry, and Cecil slept. Up front Murray was taking his turn behind the wheel, and he was listening to some country music turned down low on the car radio.

Murray reached into his pocket, took out something, and offered it to Eddie. "Want this?"

It was his transistor radio.

"Thanks." Eddie put in the earplug, settled back in his seat, and snapped it on. He listened to Ricky Nelson singing about a traveling man.

Then the announcer came on and Eddie realized he was listening to Murray the K.

"Your show's on," Eddie told Murray in the front seat.

Murray nodded. "You can change it if you want."

Eddie twirled the tuning knob and heard static and buzzing and snippets of songs. Some of the noises were kind of creepy, being a long way from home and looking out the window into the moonless nightscape. Then he stumbled across a baseball game, and when he heard the words 'Candlestick Park' he knew he had been lucky enough to find someone playing the Giants. The station went in and out, but he was able to hear in the bottom of the ninth when Willie Mays knocked in a run and won the game.

He thought of his classmates playing in the Sand Mountain league this year and how they all got their own uniforms. He would have tried out for second base. He would be like a brick wall on the right side of the infield. Nothing would get past him. Eddie imagined himself warming up in the on-deck circle, swinging two bats at once to loosen up. "Look out, now," the old timers would say in the stands. "Kandy Kane's boy is stepping up to the plate."

He snapped the radio off, yawned, and handed it up to Murray.

"What's that music called you said you played up in New York?"

"We played all kinds of things," Murray said, smiling as he remembered. "Sunday afternoons we all gather at Washington Square and just have a big hootenanny all day long. There's fiddles and guitars and banjos and penny whistles. There's a guy there playing bongos all the time. Twelve string guitars. They really fill up the sound. You hear old folk songs, and some blues, and some calypso. And it all gets mixed up together. It's really boss."

Murray rolled his head on his shoulders and Eddie could hear his bones pop. "Take the banjo. People keep borrowing it back and forth. The slaves brought it over from Africa. They stuck a neck on a gourd, put some strings on it, and plunked away. Our folks–white folks–never heard of a banjo till the slaves starting playing them. But then, after a while, the banjo became something we played. It's an instrument that's been taken over by white folks. I've seen a lot of great banjo players–you'd be surprised how that little African instrument has worked its way into the New York scene–and I've jammed at Washington Square with Pete Seeger and Winnie Winston and Eric Weissberg–but I've never seen a Negro play the five-string banjo. Same thing with a fiddle. You read old stories about the plantations in the South, and there's always something about the music. The slaves played all sorts of dance tunes on the fiddle. Now, I've seen classically trained colored musicians play the violin in an orchestra. But I've never seen a Negro play old fiddle tunes. It makes me wonder who will be playing the banjo and the fiddle a hundred years from now. Probably not a Jewish kid from New York or a kid from Sand Mountain."

Eddie leaned on the back of the front seat, resting his head on his folded arms. "Murray, what's an integrationist?"

"An integrationist believes folks should be together."

"Like how?"

Murray looked at the other men in the car and saw that they were still sleeping. He lowered his voice. "Well, some people–a lot of people down here in the South–believe that we ought to stay separate. Colored people shouldn't have anything to do with white people, and vice versa. But other folks think that's wrong. They want to integrate schools. They think all kinds of kids should go to school together."

"And now they want to integrate buses?" Eddie asked, remembering the sign.

Murray nodded. "They think it's wrong that colored people have to sit in the back of the bus and use different waiting rooms."

Eddie thought of Martha Gale, the only girl in his whole school who wore braces. When she was at the front of the bus, he sat in back. When she sat in the back, he sat up front. Martha Gale made him nervous. "What's so terrible about everyone sitting where they want on the bus?"

"It's different from what people are used to."

"Do they have integrationists in New York City?"

Murray laughed. "We've always been mixed up there. If you tried separating people in New York you'd run out of places to put them. I went to school with Irish kids, Puerto Ricans, kids from China. I played stickball all the time with a bunch of colored guys who had moved from South Carolina. And there's lots of us Jewish kids up there, too."

Jewish? Eddie thought. I've never known a real, live Jewish person on Sand Mountain before.

That was the last thing he thought about before he fell asleep.

CHAPTER VII

Devil's Dream

One morning the air smelled different when Eddie woke up. It was sweet and substantial. He took a deep breath and filled his lungs and it was like taking a big bite of an apple. He rose, looked out the window, and saw a beautiful carpet of green trees gently sloping to the sky. "Where are we?" he asked, rubbing his eyes.

"Back home," said his uncle Berry. "That's Sand Mountain."

Eddie sat on the edge of the seat. "Home?"

Berry was driving now. Apparently they had stopped somewhere in the night because Murray was at the wheel the night before. "Yeah, we're back in Alabama. But we don't have time to stop and visit your folks. We're doing a show at the VFW in Montgomery."

Eddie sat back in the seat, leaned over, and

pressed his cheek against the cold window. Momma and Daddy are right over there, he thought, but I can't see them. He tried to remember how long it had been since he had left home, but it was just an endless string of days and nights, sitting in the car and then playing for strangers. For a while, hamburgers every night for supper had been fun. Now he was tired of the heavy, thick air that seemed to fill every diner where the silverware clanked and the grill splattered grease. And he'd ordered eggs and grits for breakfast every morning they had time to stop, but the eggs were always too runny or too dry or too cold and the grits were lumpy and tasteless. He missed his mother's cooking. He missed home.

A few nights after he had trouble getting the right change in the pay phone he started to call her again, but he hung up as soon as he heard the dial tone. He was so homesick he knew he'd start crying once he heard her, and he didn't want her to hear that.

Eddie didn't know if he could stand doing this all summer, no matter how badly his daddy needed the money for the farm.

It didn't take long to heat up, and by the time they got beyond Sand Mountain they had rolled down all the windows. "You think it's hot here, just wait till we get to Montgomery," Cecil said, wiping his face with his handkerchief. "Hottest city in Dixie. You'll see."

Their route took them through Birmingham, a big, noisy city full of steel mills and foundries and railroads, a place unlike the rest of the South Eddie had seen in his travels. Eddie strained to look up at the tall buildings downtown, and marveled at the wide streets choked with cars and the sidewalks full of Saturday shoppers. They drove past long trains pulling endless chains of cars filled with big lumps of coal. Everywhere Eddie looked smokestacks poked into the sky, belching huge clouds of black smoke. The air was acrid and foul from the foundries and steel mills.

"Smell that?" Cecil said up front. "Smells like money."

Eddie took a deep breath and wrinkled his nose. It smelled like rotten eggs. If you lived here you'd have to keep the windows on the car rolled up, no matter how hot it got. And it was plenty hot, even though it was only May. Eddie frowned when he thought of spending the entire summer broiling in the back seat of the car. Why couldn't his uncles get air conditioning?

Everything in the city seemed to be coated with the black dust and grime from the foundries. South of Birmingham on Highway 31, though, it was just the opposite. They passed trucks and trees and buildings white as ghosts and every now and then smokestacks behind huge mounds of earth pumped pure white into the sky. It looked to Eddie as if they were making clouds.

"Limestone," Murray said, reading his mind. "They quarry limestone around here. That little town we passed through, Calera. Calera means 'limestone' in Spanish."

Soon the black and white world turned golden

as they drove past orchards full of small trees with twisted limbs loaded with fruit. Peaches, Eddie realized. I'd love to have some of Momma's peach cobbler right now. He pictured two scoops of vanilla ice cream melting over a big piece.

Eddie had seen a picture of the state capitol in Montgomery on a calendar at Doyle's Gas Station back home, but when he looked up at Goat Hill and saw that brilliant white dome against the deep blue sky he thought it was the most magnificent thing he had ever seen. He knew what it was because he recognized the Alabama state flag–a big red "X" on a white rectangle.

"Turn here," Byron said to his brother, who was driving. "I think the VFW is to the south."

They passed one building after another with huge stone columns. Men in bronze and marble and granite stood watch in front of the state government buildings, some armed with a musket, some with a book. "Knowledge," Eddie said softly, reading aloud the words he saw carved above the entry to a building. "Liberty."

"Justice."

Berry hesitated at an intersection and then turned left. The buildings were smaller now, and Eddie saw the sign of the sprinting dog he'd seen posted at gas stations and truck stops along every highway they had traveled. It was the Greyhound bus depot.

"What in Sam Hill. . ." Berry began, but he didn't finish the sentence. Through the open window Eddie caught a whiff of diesel fumes and something burning. In front of them they saw a mob gathering around one of the buses. People were running and yelling. Someone darted off the bus and Eddie saw a brick in the air then one of the huge windows in the front of the building shattered. Then, pow! pow!, two men swinging clubs broke two windows on a car. They heard laughter, cries, screams, and the crash of rocks and clubs knocking on the side of the bus. Four white boys, all of them with crew-cuts and wearing t-shirts, were chasing a colored man across the parking lot. One of the boys carried a baseball bat. He swung it and the man they were chasing dropped and he didn't get up. Another man scampered to a trash pile and picked up a wooden crate. He smashed it over the colored man's head.

Over by the bus Eddie saw a white boy sitting on top of a Negro man who was stretched out on the parking lot. He was hitting him with both fists, beating the living daylights out of him. The man raised himself on one elbow and tried to protect himself with his other arm, but the boy kept pummelling him. People ran past. No one stopped to help.

Behind the bus a colored man squatted, trying to hide from the others. He covered his mouth with both hands, and his white short-sleeve shirt was streaked with a red X from the blood that was pouring from between his fingers. He looked up and saw Eddie and the others. He raised up, perhaps to approach them.

"Go! Go!" Cecil shouted.

As if he were waiting for instructions, Berry

hit the accelerator and turned the steering wheel sharply. Eddie could hear the bass fiddle on the roof scrape and groan under the strain. Berry braked and turned around to pick his way around parked cars and people dashing across the street. A man and a woman, sprinting toward the bus station, darted in front of them and Berry had to stomp on the brake. The man quickly looked at them, stopped to beat on the hood as if it were a drum, and then let out a rebel yell. "Yee haw!" he screamed, tilting his head back. The woman with him laughed. Berry had hardly gotten the car moving again when everyone inside was startled by a loud thud behind them. They all turned and saw that a man had been shoved into the back of their car and then had fallen to the ground. His bloody hand left a single perfect fingerprint on the window. Murray reached for the door—he wasn't going to open it, was he? Eddie wondered—but Cecil grabbed his wrist.

"It's the Freedom Riders!" Murray cried.

"I said let's get out of here!" Cecil shouted at Berry.

Berry grabbed the wheel with both hands and gunned the motor. At the first intersection he ran a red light, eager to put as much distance as possible between them and the horrible scene.

When he finally pulled over in a church parking lot a couple of minutes later, no one said a word. It was as if they had all had a terrible dream and they didn't want to acknowledge it by speaking of it. All was quiet, except for an occasional passing car and the cat-call of a mockingbird, which Eddie could see in a chinaberry tree in the church yard. He looks just like a Sand Mountain mockingbird, Eddie thought. They were mean birds and would swoop down and attack a cat or sometimes even a person for no reason. Eddie was short of breath and could feel his heart beating fast. He turned away from the bird and saw the fingerprint on the car window, clearly visible against the white stones of the church building, and almost threw up. He looked at Murray to ask him what was going on, what happened back there. But he saw that Murray's eyes were red, and he was using the heel of his hand to brush away tears. So he didn't say anything.

CHAPTER VIII

Good Times
Are
Past and Gone

They finally found the VFW building several blocks away and Berry backed the old car to the front door so they could unload their gear. As soon as they stopped Murray hurried away like he had something important to do. Eddie suspected he just wanted to be alone. Berry's hands were shaking, Eddie noticed, as Cecil and he struggled with the rope that secured the bass to the top of the car. Eddie walked into the building with Byron. His uncle's jaw jutted, like he was working on something, chewing on something. He rubbed the back of his neck, and then took off his Stetson hat and ran a hand through his hair. He shook his head and then pushed the hat back on. He walked to a corner of the room where a single microphone was set up. He blew into it and the sound reverberated in the room. Byron turned away from the mike and grimaced. Eddie's daddy always laughed and said Berry was the excitable one, and Byron was the steady one. Eddie had never seen his uncle this agitated.

The VFW post was an old, grimy building with dingy, scuffed linoleum floors. Eddie could see from posters that they were playing at a covered dish supper. If I lived in a big city like Montgomery I'd take my momma out to eat every weekend, he thought. I wouldn't make her fix nothing.

A few folks had already arrived, and Eddie could smell the fried chicken and cornbread they had brought. He surveyed the table and saw deviled eggs and potato salad and baked beans. Macaroni and cheese and sliced tomatoes. Cucumbers and slices of cantaloupe. Cakes and pies and brownies. But it made him a little sick to his stomach. He couldn't get out of his mind the white shirt with the red stain. And the fingerprint.

The other members of the band joined Eddie and his uncle, and they gathered in a storage closet off the main room and wordlessly tuned up. Why isn't anyone saying anything? he wanted to ask. But since no one was talking, he couldn't. Eddie could hear the scrape of chairs and the shuffling of feet beyond the door and he reckoned the crowd was gathering.

They were introduced and from the start they had problems. First Cecil knocked over the microphone with the bass when he stepped up to sing a solo, and the speaker system wailed and everyone covered their ears. Then Berry broke a guitar string and Cecil told some jokes to kill time while Berry made the repair, but no one laughed. It seemed to Eddie as if the people were distracted and didn't care to listen to them at all. There was a lot of talk and shuffling, and little kids raced around the chairs. Byron forgot the words to a song he was singing–that had never happened, as far as Eddie knew–and the band had to vamp on the chord until Murray prompted him.

Then Byron introduced him as The Twelve-Year-Old Terror of the Five String Banjo. While his uncle struggled with the mike to move it closer to his banjo, Eddie stole a look at the crowd and he almost fainted. Over there, at that back table, wasn't that the laughing woman who had walked in front of their car by the bus depot? He looked away, afraid to confirm his suspicions. As he glanced at Murray to see if anything registered with him, Eddie froze. That guy in the t-shirt–was he the one with the baseball bat? The room started spinning and his knees buckled. He tried to swallow, but his mouth felt like it was stuffed with cotton. If it hadn't been for the music kicking off at that exact moment he might have passed out. But the thumping of the bass jolted him and, like it was some kind of reflex, he began playing.

But not very well.

His fingers felt like they were frozen and he couldn't make them move on his solo. The band kept going but there was an empty space where he should have been playing. Everyone in the band looked at him, expecting him to do something, but his fingers just wouldn't work. He bowed and studied the head of his banjo, the brilliant white top that looked like a drum, and he swore he saw a jagged, red "X" on it, like blood had spilled on it, too.

The band never recovered. They sounded out-of-tune and listless. Eddie was in a fog. He couldn't see right or hear right, and it seemed as if he were always behind the music. It was passing him by.

He thought the show would never end, but he dreaded what might happen when it did. Would his uncles get rid of him? They loved their music and worked hard to make it sound right. He thought of all those hours sitting the car, practicing with the others in the dark of the night as they hurtled down the road. It still wasn't enough. Would his uncles fire him on the spot for messing up so bad?

One thing's for sure, Eddie thought. I don't want to go home on the Greyhound.

After they were done Eddie drifted back to the storage room and pretended to be occupied with getting his banjo back in the case. He took his time before re-emerging, checking the strings, pressing on the head with his fingers to check the tension, waiting until the crowd had cleared out and the food was gone. Finally there were no more footsteps in the hall, so he hefted the banjo and made his way to the big room, the empty chairs scattered around tables covered with soiled paper tablecloths. As he stepped outside and approached the car Berry rubbed Eddie's hair and gave him a nod. "That was a rough one. For all of us."

They worked as quickly in the darkness as they could, eager to end the day's business. They piled the instrument cases in the trunk with their other belongings, and then Byron, Berry, and Cecil gave Murray their hats as they climbed into the car. He arranged them behind the back seat as always and the gravel spun under their tires as the car sped away.

That night as they drove out of town they heard on the news how the Freedom Riders had been attacked in Montgomery.

"The whole country's talking about it," Murray said. "From now on when people think of Alabama, they're going to think of what we saw today."

"It wouldn't have happened if all them Yankees had stayed home and minded their own business," Cecil said, shaking his head, and quickly changing to another station.

Yankees? Eddie thought. Like Mantle and Whitey Ford and Roger Maris, remembering the players he'd watched on TV with his daddy.

"It wouldn't have happened if the law had been obeyed," Murray shot back. "They took the law in their own hands. That's not what America's about."

"Don't tell me what America's about," Cecil said, his face getting red.

"All right, you two," Byron said, holding up his hands. "That's enough. We've got to work together. And judging from tonight we've got a long way to go."

Berry quickly reached for his mandolin and began tuning it. "Let's work on 'Toy Heart,'" he said.

But Byron shook his head. "Not tonight. We need a break. Let's just sit back and take it easy for a while."

The earth had been baking in the sun all day long, and all four windows on the old car were about halfway down—enough to stir the air, but not so much that everyone inside would be blown away. The warm wind roared about them as they rushed down the highway.

"Seems like she's flying tonight," Berry said.

Byron nodded. "Yeah, the old chariot is really rolling up some real estate for a change."

Eddie closed his eyes and tried to sleep, but he was restless. What a day.

Sometime later he felt the car lurch and opened his eyes to see that Byron had pulled off the road. "We all need to cool off," he said, bringing the car to a halt. "Let's bivouac here for a while. Maybe the night air will do us some good."

They had stopped at a roadside park. Eddie could see it had a concrete picnic table and a historical marker, but it was too dark to read it. He wasn't sure what it meant to "bivouac," but he hoped it didn't mean he was going to have to play the banjo. His fingers were sore and his back hurt.

Byron opened the trunk and rummaged around for a bit. He dug out a couple of blankets, gathered

Raising Kane

them in his arms, and then walked around the car and laid them across the hood and front window. "Why don't you two take the master bedroom," he said, nodding at Murray and Eddie.

They climbed up on the car, reclined against the window, and stuck their feet out in front of them down by the hood ornament. Eddie turned around and saw Cecil was lying in the front seat, his feet hanging out the window on the passenger's side, and Berry was across the back seat. Byron walked away from them and sat down against a tree, his knees pulled up to his chest.

Murray drew up a leg and reached to pull off one of his cowboy boots. "Ahh," he sighed, wiggling his toes. "That feels better."

"Ya'll sit still up there," Cecil grumbled. Murray rolled his eyes but was careful not to rock the car when he pulled off his other boot.

Eddie's eyes gradually adjusted to the darkness. I bet I could read that historical marker now, he thought, but he decided he'd better stay put. He put his hands behind his head and looked at the sky. There was no moon, so thousands of stars were plainly visible, the brightest of them brilliant, blazing points of white in the deep, black sky. "I see both dippers and the Seven Little Sisters," he whispered to Murray, recognizing the few stars he could name.

"I don't know any stars," Murray said. "It's too light in the city where I grew up. You can't see anything in the sky except planes."

Eddie took a deep breath, exhaled, and crossed

his legs. I'm glad I grew up where you can see the stars, he thought.

Murray continued scanning the sky. "Eddie, did you ever wonder how things got this way?"

Eddie wanted to answer him. But he couldn't decide if Murray was talking about the stars in the sky or what happened at the bus station that afternoon.

CHAPTER IX

Soldier's Joy

Eddie was the last one to wake, and he was surprised to see daylight. When he fell asleep the night before he was sure they were just taking a nap, that someone would roust him in a couple of hours while it was still dark and they'd be on their way, practicing again in the car. Instead, when he rubbed his eyes open and swung his feet off the side of the car he heard the morning birds singing, saw a red sun low on the horizon, and found Berry, Byron, Cecil, and Murray standing in a tight knot.

"The last time I saw it, it was on the sidewalk in front of the VFW," Cecil said. "It was dark when we left, you know, so I guess we just drove off with it like that."

"What do you mean 'we'?" asked Berry. "Everyone's responsible for his own instrument.

If I left my mandolin somewhere it wouldn't be anyone's fault but mine."

"You can't compare a mandolin and a big bull fiddle like that!" said Cecil. "You know with my lumbago I can't get it on and off the car by myself."

Byron walked quickly to the front of the car and gathered the blankets off the hood. "Oh, shut up, both of you." He stuffed the blankets through the back window of the car. "The quicker we leave, the quicker we get back."

Without another word he got behind the steering wheel. Berry and Cecil hurried into the car as Byron started it and revved the engine. Then the big car did a u-turn, creating a huge plume of dust, and took off down the road, back the way they had come last night.

Eddie and Murray watched the car disappear. Then Murray stuck his hands in his pockets and started whistling.

Eddie had always been a slow riser. Sometimes his mother had to call him three or four times to get him out of bed on school days, especially those winter mornings when it was still dark and he knew the wooden floor would be ice cold. He wasn't very talkative in the morning: he had to ease into the day. So he was a little slow to understand what exactly was happening to him at this roadside park just after sun-up. "Murray, have we been fired or something?"

"No sir," Murray answered, resuming his whistling.

"Well, what's going on?"

Murray backed onto a picnic table and then

lifted his feet and placed them on the bench. "Remember last night when your uncles were talking about how well the old car was driving, how fast it was zipping down the road?"

Eddie shrugged. He remembered something like that.

"Well, we just had a physics lesson. Cecil's bass fiddle creates a lot of drag when it's on top of the car. It's like driving down the road pulling a parachute."

Eddie covered his mouth with an open hand. "The bass fiddle's gone!"

Murray began laughing and clapping his hands. "Cecil thinks he left it on the sidewalk in front of the VFW!" he said, rocking back and forth. "Yes, sir, Cecil, that's mighty fine! Mighty fine!"

Eddie slowly sat on the bench beside Murray's feet. "What now?"

"They've gone back to get it, though who knows where it is by now."

"What are we supposed to do?"

"There's a little town called Eminence about two miles down the road. I talked your uncles into letting us stay."

"Why?"

"Well, I told them that you'd been gone a long time and you still haven't called your mother and she was going to be mad—really mad— if she didn't hear from you." Murray slid to his feet and looked at the sun and looked down the road, away from Montgomery. "And, to tell you the truth, I was beginning to think that if I didn't get a day off from sitting in that car I was going to die. Let's go."

Side by side they set out on the open road. Eddie couldn't tell where they were. It was awfully flat and there was nothing but pine trees all around. "You reckon we're still in Alabama?"

"Don't you recognize this?" Murray said, his hand sweeping in front of him. "This is Hank's Lost Highway!"

Eddie just looked at him.

"Hank Williams! You've heard of Hank Williams up on Sand Mountain, haven't you?"

Eddie nodded. Everybody knew a Hank Williams song or two. "Your Cheatin' Heart." "Kaw-liga." "I Saw the Light."

"If he got lost on this highway, maybe it's not such a good place for us."

"Byron said they'd pick us up at the drug store this afternoon."

"Which one?"

"A town this size will only have one."

"Eddie, is that you?"

"Yes, Momma, it's me."

"Why has it taken so long for us to hear from you?" she asked sharply. "I've been worried sick."

"I tried to call," Eddie said quickly, afraid his mother was going to get mad at his uncles. "But I got mixed up with the operator and counting the change." In fact, without Murray's help with this pay phone, Eddie wouldn't have been able to place this call.

"It's good to hear you, Son," she interrupted,

her voice softer. "Where are you?"

It's called Eminence, he told her, and all he could say is that this little town looked like a hundred others he'd passed through since joining the band. There was a service station with a "We Fix Flats" sign. A barbershop with its spiraling red and white pole. A tractor company with dark green John Deeres parked in front. A dry goods store and a little grocery. A pawnshop with tarnished silverware and trays of twisted necklaces and yellowed pocket watches in the window. And a diner where he and Murray had just finished breakfast after their short walk into town. "I'm not sure where I am, Momma. I can't keep it all straight."

"That's all right. It's just good to hear from you."

"How are you? How's Daddy?"

"We're fine. Are you eating well?"

"I just had a big breakfast, Momma. But I miss your cooking."

"You'll have plenty of time to eat my cooking when you get back."

"I wish I was there now."

"You hush. There's no better place for you this summer than out on the road with your uncles. Music's in you through and through. And the money is a godsend."

"Momma, it's boring riding in the car all day. Then I have to get up in front of strangers and they're all looking at me."

"Yes, that's right. It's hard being a professional musician. I've known since you was little bitty that you had the hands for it. Now

at the end of the summer you'll know if you've
got the heart for it. If you don't, you'll come
back home and that will be the end of it. But if
your heart catches up with all the music that's
in you, there'll be no stopping you. That'll be
all you're good for."

"I like the music, Momma. It's the other
things that bother me."

"What other things?"

He paused. "We saw something terrible yesterday."

"What did you see?"

He wasn't going to tell her. He knew it would
upset her. But he couldn't help it. "We saw the
Freedom Riders. They got beat up real bad when
we passed the bus station in Montgomery."

His mother didn't say anything.

"It was terrible."

"I saw it on the television," she finally said.
"You be safe. Don't get mixed up in something
that's none of your business."

"They beat them up just because they want to
sit where they want on the bus."

"Eddie, you know there's good people, and
there's bad people. Doesn't matter if you're on
Sand Mountain or wherever you are. You be good.
That's the way we raised you."

"Yes, ma'am." It seemed to him that the
bad people had the upper hand in Montgomery
Saturday, but he didn't want to say that to his
mother. "All those men were getting beat up and
no one helped them."

His momma had no answer to that.

"Is Daddy there?"

"He's out in the fields."

"I wanted to talk some baseball with him."

"He'd like that. He watches the games, but it's not the same without you here."

They didn't talk much more because the operator came on and told him his time was up and he'd have to put in more money. He wasn't sure how to do that. So he quickly said good-bye to his mother, told her he was looking forward to getting back home, and then hung up.

"How's everyone on the farm?" asked Murray.

"Okay, I guess." He expected his mother would be a little more sympathetic about him being homesick. "She didn't say much when I told her I missed everyone."

"Of course not. That would have just made you feel bad. She's treating you like a grown up. You're not a little kid anymore. You're a professional musician out on the road and everything."

Then they swapped places and Murray began feeding coins into the pay phone. Eddie studied the front page of the local paper while Murray laughed and talked with his mother. Murray sounded different. He was using a different accent. And Eddie wasn't trying to eavesdrop, but when Murray's grandmother got on the line he began speaking an entirely different language.

Later, when they were walking through town, killing time, Eddie asked him about it.

"My grandmother's from the old country. She speaks Yiddish. You ever heard of Yiddish?"

Eddie looked at him quizzically. They walked past a broken-down pickup with a huge pig in the back. Two barefoot kids sitting on the curb poured a bag of peanuts into an RC Cola and each took a drink.

"No, I guess you wouldn't have," Murray said. "It's part Hebrew and part Polish and part German, I guess. The only time I speak the little bit I know is when I'm around my nana."

"Your what?"

"My grandmother."

"Oh." Then he remembered the accent Murray had used on the phone. "You sounded different, even when you were speaking English."

"I guess my New York accent comes out when I'm talking to them. I can usually hide it when it works to my advantage."

"You don't want to sound different down here."

"Right."

There wasn't much to do. It would be a couple of hours before his uncles and Cecil would be back. But it was so nice to be out of the car for a day and not be in a rush to get somewhere that for a while Eddie didn't notice they were being followed.

Murray did. He put his arm around Eddie's shoulder as they passed the filling station. "Come on," he said, and they hurried across the street.

So did the four men behind them. They kept their distance—they stayed about ten feet back—but wherever Eddie and Murray went, they went, too.

Finally Murray stopped in front of the barbershop. He took a deep breath, let it out slowly, and then turned around. "Good morning, gentlemen."

They didn't say anything. Three of them stood behind the largest one, a man with thick, whiskered jowls in faded overalls and a white shirt buttoned to the neck despite the considerable heat of the morning. His straw hat was pushed back and revealed a bald, sunburned head. Eddie knew a farmer's tan when he saw one, and he knew this man worked in the fields. The others struck him as townfolk, though. One was wearing a uniform that you might see on the fellow at the service station, and he had a tire pressure gauge poking out of the top of his pocket. The thin old man with thick glasses was too clean to be a farmer. There was a teenager with them, too, and Eddie thought it odd that the cuffs on his shirt were damp.

"Hot already," Murray said, pulling a red handkerchief from his pocket and wiping his brow. He looked at Eddie. "Getting hotter."

"You boys ain't from around here, are you?" said the big one.

"No, you're right. We're not."

"Well, may I ask just what it is you're doing here?"

"Sweating."

Eddie thought it was a pretty good joke, but none of the men laughed. That's when he realized this wasn't a friendly conversation.

"Bo here washes dishes at the diner," the man said, hooking his thumb and pointing it over his shoulder without looking back. "He heard you on the phone this morning. He says you wasn't talking no English."

"Is that so?"

"Yeah, that's so."

Eddie looked up at Murray and gave him a sideways nod. "Let's go," he said.

"I don't think they're finished with us," Murray said, not turning away from the man in the overalls.

"That's right. We're not finished with you. Where you from, boy?"

"New York City."

Bo spanked his hands together. "I knew it!" He elbowed the thin old man next to him. "I told you he was a foreigner!"

The man in overalls raised his hand to silence Bo. "And what brings you down here, Mr. New York City?"

"Business."

Oh, brother, Eddie thought. These guys look like they could have been at the bus station yesterday. What did Momma just tell me on the phone this morning? "Don't get mixed up in anything that's not your business."

"We was just wondering what business you're in. 'Cause if you're some kind of Northern agitator down here trying to scare up trouble, you've come to the wrong place."

"We're not scaring up any trouble," Eddie said quickly. "We're just walking around."

"I'm talking to him," the man said, his eyes not moving from Murray.

"We're just strolling," was all Murray said. "There's no law against strolling around here, is there?"

"Some agitators strolled into Montgomery yesterday and got more than they bargained for. Any agitator comes in here is gonna find the same thing."

"That's right," said the man from the filling station. The others nodded in agreement.

The man in the overalls took a step forward and then hooked his thumbs under his straps. "You don't see us going up to New York to tell your kind how to do things. What do you want to come down here for?"

Murray's eyes narrowed. He's a fighter, Eddie realized. We could get in some real trouble here. Eddie was scared. "We're in a band. We play with the Bragger Brothers," he said, trying to sound cheerful.

"Ain't no New York Jew never played no bluegrass," the man sneered. He turned to Eddie. "Where you from, boy?"

"Up on Sand Mountain."

"You better go back and get away from this one here. He's trouble."

"I'm telling you we're musicians," Eddie said, taking a step forward. "We're playing all over the place. People come from all over to hear us."

The man lifted his straw hat and wiped his forehead with a shirtsleeve. "You may say you're musicians, but I don't see no instruments. I think you're down here agitating. Both of you."

Eddie could take lots of things, but this man was calling him a liar. And there may have been good-for-nothing Braggers and ornery Braggers and hopeless Braggers. And on the other side of the family, there was talk of some uncles who had spent time at Kilby prison for running moonshine. But there never had been a liar among the Braggers or Kanes as far as Eddie knew. So, even though they were in trouble, he couldn't stand being called a liar, even by a stranger in a little, no-count town. "What if I can prove you're wrong?"

"You can't prove nothing."

"I can prove it and if you won't let me I say you're a great big chicken."

The man unhooked his thumbs from his straps and put his hands on his hips. "No one calls me a liar. I don't care how young they are."

"And no one accuses me or my friend of agitating without giving us a chance to defend ourselves."

"All right, Mr. Sand Mountain. Prove it. But if you're wrong . . ."

Eddie didn't say anything. He spun around and began walking up the street. Murray followed, and then the four men.

"I hope you've got a plan," Murray whispered. "I sure don't."

The passed the diner and the service station and the dry goods store. Every place they went a couple of people would emerge and join the others. By they time they got to the little city hall there was a parade of thirty or forty people. "Says they're musicians," Eddie could hear them laughing. "Agitators," another one said, and he could hear others agree. "Troublemakers." "Run 'em out of town." "Yankees."

Raising Kane   73

Eddie stopped at the pawn shop, opened the door, and waited for his eyes to adjust from the sunlight to the darkness of the long, narrow room. The owner sat back on a stool, chewing on a cigar. Stale, blue smoke from the stogie hung in the air. "Gotta have a fiddle and a banjo in here," Eddie whispered to Murray. "Every pawn shop's got musical instruments."

"Maybe up on Sand Mountain where everybody plays something," Murray whispered back. "By the look of things in here, these folks are hunters, not pickers."

It was true. Eddie had never seen such an assortment of shotguns and rifles and pistols. They were on racks against the wall and in glass counters in front of them. And more firearms were heaped on the counter behind the man with the cigar.

"Help you?" he said gruffly, looking at the crowd that had gathered outside his shop.

"You got a banjo and a fiddle?"

"Don't get much call for that sort of thing around these parts," the man said. But he slid off his stool, turned around, and began pushing away old radios and toasters and waffle irons and orphaned bowling shoes and hair dryers and all kinds of junk to see what he had. Finally he produced an old fiddle and a long bow and handed it to Murray.

Murray shook his head. "It's a three-quarter sized violin. A kiddie fiddle. And it's missing a string. And this is a bow for a bass fiddle. I can't play anything with this."

The man in the overalls turned to the crowd

that had gathered. "See! I told you! He can't play nothing!"

Then the pawnshop owner handed Eddie a beat-up, homemade banjo with rusty strings and a warped neck. It's the biggest piece of junk I've ever seen, Eddie thought. But it didn't matter. He slipped his right hand into his pocket, pushed on his two finger picks and the thumb pick, quickly tuned the banjo as best he could, and started "Sally Goodin.'"

At first even Eddie couldn't recognize the tune. The banjo was so old and so mistreated he figured all the music must have been beat out of it. But he kept playing. And the people stopped their talking and making fun and hushed. The banjo didn't have any oomph left in it and he couldn't get any volume out of it, so everyone leaned forward to hear. And all eyes were on him. He had to show them what he could do. He had to coax a tune out of that old banjo or there would be trouble. For him and Murray.

At the chorus the fiddle came in. Murray must have tuned while I was concentrating on getting some noise out of this sorry thing, Eddie thought. He turned slightly to Murray so more of the sound would reach him, and he saw his friend grimace as he tried to play the little fiddle with the huge bow. It looked like something you might see in a cartoon. But in spite of missing a string, in spite of everything else, Murray was making music.

It was quiet except for the music. Of all the shows we've done, I've never worked harder, Eddie thought. He could see the perspiration popping up on Murray's forehead, too. They were working like their lives depended on it.

Then he saw a foot tapping in the back of the crowd. Then another. Someone started clapping. And people began smiling and nodding and elbowing each other. The man in overalls drifted away, his head down, his hands tucked in the bib of his overalls. Momma's right, Eddie realized. There's power in music. Look what it can do.

The crowd pressed forward, eager to hear, and clapped when the song ended. "All right!" "Mighty fine!" they said. Eddie began a slow version of "Listen to the Mockingbird" because he loved how Murray could make those birdcalls on the fiddle. He also thought it would be fun to see Murray try to manage that with just three strings. Murray narrowed his eyes, like he was put out with Eddie, but it was just for show, and he did a bob white, catbird, whippoorwill, and wren on his solo. The people clapped even harder after that song, and when Eddie tried returning the banjo to the pawnshop owner the old man took the cigar out of his mouth and shook his head.

"Keep playing," he said. "It's the first time in forever we've had decent music here."

So they did a couple more songs as best they could on their ham-strung instruments. Murray did a version of "Shady Grove" that Eddie thought was as good if not better than the one he played on his fancy fiddle. Then Murray told the crowd he was going to play a solo–something Eddie didn't know–and he started a quick, exotic tune that Eddie wouldn't have been able to follow anyway. Eddie had never heard anything like it. He could tell that this fiddle song had a bunch of minor chords in it, but it didn't seem to go verse, chorus, verse, like all the other instrumentals he'd heard.

"What was that?" Eddie asked when Murray finished and the people were clapping.

"It's a klezmer tune," Murray said, pulling loose hairs off the big bow in his right hand. "That's music we play back home. It's part jazz, part dance tunes, part cantor. Do you know what a cantor is?"

"Like a horse canters?"

Murray smiled and shook his head. "When I go to temple we sing the prayers and the scriptures in Hebrew. And the guy who leads us is called the cantor." Murray thoughtfully sawed on a couple of strings while the applause died. "At least I hear a little bit of a cantor when I play these songs. There's a lot of Eastern European music in klezmer, too. It's like a soup where you throw in a bit of everything you've got in the kitchen."

"How 'bout 'Alabama?'" a woman called from the back of the crowd.

Murray went right in to it. And since it was a Louvin Brothers song, and since the Louvins were the biggest music act ever to come off Sand Mountain, Eddie knew it, too.

CHAPTER X

'Tis Sweet to Be Remembered

There was a big bass fiddle strapped to the top of the car when The Bragger Brothers drove up that afternoon, so Eddie assumed all had gone well in Montgomery.

But it hadn't.

As Berry explained, when they got to the VFW post they found a bunch of police cars parked around the building with their lights flashing. The policemen had set up barricades and wouldn't let anyone through.

"We got as close as we could and asked what was going on," Berry said, "and one of the cops told us there was a bomb planted outside the VFW. We got pretty excited when we heard the news since we had just played there. But we come to find out they thought it was Cecil's fiddle that was going to blow up. No one could figure out why a big fiddle would be on the sidewalk in front of the building, and then someone heard it ticking–Cecil's alarm clock hadn't run down– and then they decided it must be a bomb. I guess after what had happened at the bus station they felt like they couldn't take any chances.

"We tried to tell them it was our fiddle and there wasn't any bomb or anything like that, but they wouldn't believe us. So they put us in the back of a squad car and took us to police headquarters for questioning.

"You should have seen all the reporters there. After the Freedom Riders got beat up at the bus station, I guess every newspaper from all over the country sent someone down to see what was going on. We told the detectives that we are in a band, that we just happened to leave a bass fiddle there. And there's a clock inside of it, we tried to tell them. But I've got to admit, it's not a very convincing story."

He raised his voice and looked at Cecil. "I mean, how can you leave a big bull fiddle sitting on the sidewalk? So they asked us about that, and asked if we had anything to do with what had happened at the bus station. And they asked us over and over and over. Well, they never did believe us, so finally they had the fire department soak the fiddle real good, I guess to wet the dynamite they thought was in it, and then some guy from the army cut a peephole in the back of the fiddle and shined a flashlight in there to make sure it wasn't going to blow up. So now we've got a water-logged, air-conditioned bull fiddle. Thanks to a certain someone," he said, looking once more at Cecil.

To make matters worse, the band had lost its next engagement. They were supposed to play at a school gymnasium that night, but the promoter said everyone was nervous because of the unrest in Montgomery and he was canceling the show.

"So we're stuck for a while," Byron said. "Our next show is not too far from here. It doesn't hardly make sense to go back home. We'd have to get back in the car as soon as we got there."

Eddie knew his uncles couldn't afford to lose many engagements, but he was glad they were getting another night off.

It was late in the day and everyone was hungry, so Berry asked if there was a diner in town where they could get something to eat.

"Follow me," Murray said, and as the band made its way along Main Street people came up to them on the sidewalk and shook their hands and slapped them on the back. One man rushed out of the barbershop, his face lathered and the cape tied around his neck. "That was the best pickin' I've heard in a long, long time!" he said, pumping Eddie's hand. When they passed the small grocery store they heard a knocking at the window and saw the butcher, his apron splattered red, smiling at them and giving them an "OK" sign.

"Looks like you two made a lot of friends," Berry said.

"Yeah, but we did it the hard way," Murray replied. "I'll tell you about it."

The lunch special that afternoon was fried

chicken, sliced tomatoes, macaroni and cheese, squash and onions, cornbread, and peach cobbler for dessert. They washed it down with sweet tea and Murray finished his story just as they pushed back their plates and began sipping steaming cups of hot coffee.

Eddie didn't care for coffee, so he had another glass of tea.

"You really picked your way out of a jam this morning, didn't you?" Byron asked Eddie when Murray had finished his story.

"I reckon."

"Were you nervous?"

"At first. But then I could see that the music was taking hold."

"You know what?" Byron had been leaning back in his chair, but sat up and put his elbows on the table. "It's time you got an Open Road."

So they got up, paid, and walked to the dry goods store two doors down.

As soon as they opened the door, Eddie could smell denim and leather. New blue jeans and overalls were stacked on the tables, and narrow aisles had been made between racks of cotton blouses, dresses, and jumpers. The shoe department was back along one wall and Eddie could see stacks of white boxes and row after row of cowboy boots, work boots, dress shoes, and white P.F. Flyer tennis shoes. A new saddle was cinched to a sawhorse beside a display case of Barlow pocketknives. "Can I help you?" the clerk said. He was wearing a western shirt and a belt with a big silver buckle.

"The young man needs a Stetson Open Road,"

Byron said.

"A Stetson Open Road," the man repeated, and they followed him to shelves brimming with hatboxes. The man tried a couple of hats on Eddie before he settled on one. The third one was a little loose, but the clerk seemed satisfied.

"Go look in the mirror," the man said, steering Eddie by the shoulders. "See what you think."

Eddie stepped in front of a three-paneled mirror so he could almost see completely around himself. It was a beautiful hat, just like the ones Byron, Berry, and Murray wore. It wasn't exactly a cowboy hat. The brim was short and the crown was higher. It looked like the kind of hat you might wear if you owned a big ranch and had lots of cowboys working for you. The Stetson Open Road was the signature of The Bragger Brothers.

"I like it," Eddie said, beaming.

"It's a little loose," the clerk said, "but you'll grow into it."

"Ring it up," said Byron.

Eddie pulled the hat off his head, looked inside of it, and made a sweep with his fingers of the smooth, cool leather headband. Then he saw the price tag. Twenty-seven dollars! That was a fortune!

But the clerk only rang up $13.50 at the cash register. "We're having a special sale today," he said, pushing the buttons. It seemed like the whole building shook when the drawer of the old brass cash register opened. "Anyone who puts Sterling Waters in his place gets half off."

Eddie and Murray exchanged glances.

"Sterling Waters is always trying to cause a commotion, like he tried to do with you two this morning. Those poor boys who follow him don't know any better. That's why I'm glad you came to town." He put the receipt inside the hatbox and then handed it to Eddie. "I'll bet you'd like to wear it, huh?"

"Yes, sir."

That afternoon when the big car pulled out of town there were not three but four Stetson hats lined up in the back window.

"Now it's your job to keep up with the hats," Murray told him. "Newest man in the band is always the one to keep up with the hats."

It sounded to Eddie like a rule Murray had just made up. But he didn't mind. He was happy to have his Stetson. And he was happy to be getting out of Eminence.

CHAPTER XI

River Of Jordan

"Boys, I want to be cleansed."

They were headed across the Black Belt, a strip of fertile, black soil that bisects Alabama. Ever so often they would pass through a one-stoplight town with little more than a post office and a filling station. Between towns Eddie had been staring out the window at gently rolling fields covered with cotton or soybeans. Berry was going over a new song called "Bury Me Beneath The Willow," showing Eddie and Murray exactly how he wanted the breaks to fall. But Eddie didn't need to look at the neck of his banjo anymore to know where the frets were. He gazed out the window at the passing tin-roofed shacks, wringer washing machines, and busted cane chairs on the sagging porches. The fingers on both of his hands moved on their own now, it seemed. He didn't have to coax the music out. It came on its own.

Byron slowed the car in the first town of any size they'd seen that afternoon. What kind of cleansing does he have in mind? Eddie wondered.

"The bass fiddle's clean," Murray said, not looking up from his mandolin. "The Montgomery police took care of that for us."

Cecil was in the front seat and flipped down the sun visor so he could see Murray in the mirror. "I've just about had it with you and your smart-aleck remarks!"

"Hush up, both of you," Berry said. "Do something," he told Byron. "We've been in this car 'way too long."

Byron looked left and right down side streets as the car slowly rolled through intersections. "Got to be one around here somewhere," he said to himself. Then he spotted what he was looking for, put on the blinker, and turned right. "We've been on the road too long without washing out our socks."

They pulled in at the All-Right Dry Cleaners and Winslow Washeteria, and Berry was out of the car and hurrying into the place before the car even stopped.

Cecil sniffed. "We are getting pretty ripe." He looked back at Murray. "Some of us more than others."

Then Berry leaned out the door of the building and waved them in.

"Hats, please," Murray said.

Eddie reached behind the back seat and

retrieved the hats one-by-one. As they got out of the car Byron unlocked the trunk and everyone reached in for their shaving kits and travel bags.

Eddie's stuff was in a wrinkled grocery sack.

As they filed in, Eddie heard Byron tell his brother that they were in luck. There was a shower in the back they could use.

"Afternoon," they said to the girl at the cash register. Eddie thought she was probably a high school student working afternoons. She had a short blonde ponytail, a beautiful smile, and was wearing a letter sweater. Her boyfriend was probably Big Man On Campus.

She nodded an indifferent greeting. "Right back through there," she said, pointing at a door behind the counter. Her eyes met Eddie's, and he quickly looked away.

He followed the rest of the band into a steamy, noisy, windowless room with a huge hot water heater and lots of pipes. He could hear machinery clanking and people talking on the other side of a thin wall. "Now what?" he asked.

Murray began unbuttoning his shirt. "Now you're going to see how a band on the road does laundry."

Eddie stood speechless as the other men took off everything but their Stetsons. They threw their garments in a big pile on the floor and then wrapped themselves in towels they pulled out of their bags. Eddie turned away. One of the things he worried about sometimes at night, looking out the car window into the darkness, was having to dress out for gym in front of the other guys when he got to high school. But that was two years away.

"Shake a leg," Berry told him. "We've got to get back on the road."

Eddie was embarrassed, but none of the men paid any attention as he hustled out of his clothes and threw them in with the others.

Cecil lay on a wooden table and took a nap. Murray found an old newspaper, upended a washtub, and then sat and began working the crossword puzzle. Berry and Byron found a couple of folding chairs and sat down. Berry pulled off his hat, took a deck of cards he always kept under it, and began shuffling on a paper towel box that came up to their knees. "Open the door and push those clothes out in the hall, would you?" he asked, not looking at Eddie. "She'll come get everything."

Eddie cracked the door open as much as he dared, afraid the girl at the counter would see him. He wrapped his towel around his waist, but he was so skinny there was nothing for it to hang on. He pushed the clothing out into the hall with his right foot and held on to his towel with both hands.

"It's not exactly a shower," Berry said, surveying his cards. "It's a janitor's sink with a hose. But it has hot water. Leave some for the rest of us. She said there's a bar of soap there."

Eddie made a pretty big mess, squirting himself with the hose, trying to get clean. But there was a drain in the floor so he guessed it didn't matter. It felt good, he decided, so he took his time and even washed behind his ears without his mother telling him. When he was finished the others took turns getting cleaned up. About an hour later there was a knock on the door.

"Your clothes are ready," the girl called. "I'll set them by the door."

Eddie gave her a couple of minutes to get back to the counter, then he opened the door, stuck his head out to make sure the coast was clear, and then reached for the clothing.

He didn't know how it happened, but he felt a push and he fell into the hall, his towel down at his ankles. The door slammed behind him. Horrified that the girl would see him standing in nothing but his Stetson, he wheeled about and frantically tried the knob.

Locked!

"Hey! Let me in!" he whispered urgently. If she heard him screaming she might come back to investigate. He leaned over to grab the towel and his hat fell off. He reached for it and the towel fluttered in one hand, once again leaving him exposed.

"Hey, Miss!" Cecil yelled from the other side of the door, raising his voice, trying to imitate Eddie. "Come back here a minute! There's something I want to show you!" He laughed.

Eddie crammed the hat back on his head and struggled to get both hands on the towel. "Let me in! Please!" He checked over his shoulder, sure that any second she was going to appear at the end of the hall and see him. "Open up!"

"Do it," he finally heard someone say.

"Make me!"

"Listen to me. Open that door or I'm going to run my fiddle bow in one ear and out the other!"

It seemed to Eddie like an eternity, but finally the door opened and he hurried inside, using his feet to scoot the clean clothes, which were wrapped in paper, across the floor.

"This is the dullest band I've ever been in," Cecil said, sitting in a chair and crossing his legs. "Ya'll aren't any fun at all."

Ignoring Cecil, Byron got up and took the package to his makeshift card table. He opened it and found his undershorts and t-shirt. "I feel renewed," he finally said.

"Amen, Brother," Berry added.

Eddie had to admit that it felt awfully good to be wearing some clean clothes and smelling soap and shampoo instead of sweat when they got back in the car.

As they drove away Eddie realized there had been a patch shaped like a big, white baseball sewn on that girl's letter sweater at the dry cleaner's. Girls always went for baseball players, he sighed.

CHAPTER XII

Don't Let Your Deal Go Down

Maybe it was the Stetson. Maybe it was having a day off. Or maybe something got washed away at the cleaners. Whatever it was, not too long after that they played a gig at a big farm implement store sale and Eddie realized he wasn't nervous or frightened. He even thought he saw a couple of girls in the crowd looking at him. He didn't care who was watching anymore.

How long had it been since he'd gotten his Open Road, Eddie wondered. Weeks? A month? He couldn't keep track of time, spending all day and night in the car. He remembered playing at a couple of drive-ins and at a bowling alley where it was hard to hear the music over the falling pins. They played for the opening of a new bank somewhere Eddie couldn't remember and at a catfish house where they arrived too late to eat and had to leave too quickly to gobble down even a single hushpuppy. The crowd went crazy at a big party where a sheriff was running for re-election, but Murray told him don't get the big head, it was just because everyone was likkered up on the sheriff's dime. He'd seen state line signs for Georgia and Mississippi pass in a blur but it all looked the same to him. Sometimes it was flat, sometimes it was hilly, and every now and then you'd see a little town. Eddie thought they'd gone through Birmingham once or twice, but usually Murray just shrugged when he asked where they were. Once in a blue moon his uncles would splurge and they'd spend the night in a rundown rooming house, two to a bed and one bathroom for everyone on the entire floor. However long it had been since he'd gotten the Stetson, he knew there had been a lot of sleeping in the car, eating at greasy spoons, and backseat jam sessions. And once a week they'd have to turn around and hightail it for Bristol so they could make The Early Morning Weekly Wake-Up Radio Show.

They spent the night sleeping in the car at a truck stop parking lot. The next morning they dropped in unannounced at a tiny radio station out on the highway, and Berry tried to talk the DJ into letting them sing a couple of songs live. When the man expressed his reluctance, Berry took a five-dollar bill out of his wallet and pressed it into his hand.

"That's what you call public relations," Murray whispered to Eddie.

The DJ pushed on his earphones and rolled

his chair up to the microphone.

"We're The Bragger Brothers," Berry said. "Make sure you get the name right."

The DJ admired the five-dollar bill and then grinned. "I know who you are. You've played every country crossroads in the state this summer. Every day I get someone calling me and asking to hear one of your records. You boys got any records?"

"Not yet," Berry said. "But it won't be long."

The DJ held up a finger to silence them and then flipped a switch on the console. An 'ON AIR' sign began flashing. "It's eleven forty-five, just fifteen minutes away from the farm market report, brought to you by your local Co-Op agricultural products dealer. But right now we've got an extra special treat as The Bragger Brothers have stopped by the studio and are tuning up to play a couple of songs for us."

Some studio, Eddie thought. They were all crowded behind the console with the disc jockey, leaning in towards the single microphone. It was kind of like playing in a phone booth. They kicked off "Salty Dog," which sounded pretty good despite a sort of mushy sound that came from Cecil's waterlogged bass fiddle. Eddie noticed a puddle forming under it. Still waterlogged after all this time!

That afternoon they stopped at a little grocery store and after a lot of convincing with the owner, Byron was able to make a long-distance call on his phone. Everyone else got something to eat. Eddie got an RC Cola and cheese crackers. Murray got a Moonpie and a bottle of Squirt.

"I'd rather have an egg crème and a knish," he said, paying the proprietor for their food. "But I reckon this will have to do."

They went outside and sat on the edge of the porch. Cecil sauntered out a few minutes later, a carton raised to his lips. When he lowered it he had a buttermilk moustache.

"I don't see how you can drink that stuff!" Murray frowned.

"Boy, you don't know what's good." He took another drink, sighed with satisfaction, and walked away.

Eddie waited until Cecil was leaning against the car, out of earshot. "That was the first thing you two have said to each other since you threatened him with your fiddle bow."

Murray shrugged.

Eddie nibbled on cracker, making it last. "What was that you were asking for in there?"

"An egg crème and knish?" Murray took a drink of Squirt, a grapefruit soda that came in a green bottle. "An egg crème is kind of a chocolate soda. And a knish is a great, big french fry, more or less."

"Is that stuff you ate in New York?"

He nodded, and Eddie wondered if he were homesick, too. "New York's a long way away, isn't it?"

A ragged stray slowly approached and indifferently sniffed Murray's left boot. He watched the dog walk away and collapse in the shade of rusted car in some weeds in front of the store. "Yeah. A long way away," he answered.

"How'd you end up down here in the band?"

Murray pushed up with one hand to get a more comfortable perch on the porch. "I was in school and got interested in old fiddle tunes while I was taking a folklore class. I heard about this big fiddle contest in North Carolina–Fiddler's Grove. So when the weekend for the contest came I hitched my way down there. Fiddlers from all over go there."

"Did you enter?"

He shook his head. "I was just there to learn some new tunes. But there was jamming at night around the campfires, all night long. And your uncle Byron was there jamming, too. After a few songs he turned to me and said he was looking for a fiddler and asked if I wanted to ride back with him to Alabama and join The Bragger Brothers."

"You went right back to Sand Mountain with him? You didn't even go back home to New York?"

"Haven't been back yet," he grinned sheepishly. "It didn't go over too well when I called home and told them I was quitting college to play in a bluegrass band. It's been about a year now." He chewed on his lip for a moment and narrowed his eyes. "It might be safe for me to go back in another few months." Murray stopped and leaned toward the store. "You hear your uncle?"

Eddie listened for minute. He could hear Berry talking about how the man at the radio station had been getting calls about them, asking for their music. "Yeah. I hear him."

Eddie finished the Squirt and stood to put the empty in a rack on the porch. "Your Uncle Berry is doing some public relations with Mr. Monroe."

That night they played at a cakewalk in a tiny school out in the country. After their usual hour show, the principal arranged about a dozen chairs in a circle as one of the teachers took up money. "The first one's for a lemon crackle cake that Myrtle Lawson brought in," he said, and the first dozen contestants were admitted to the circle.

Then Berry spoke. "Before we begin I want to announce publicly for the first time that The Bragger Brothers have just been invited to appear with Bill Monroe at his big tent show in Middleburg, Florida."

Byron and Cecil didn't change expressions, but Murray smiled when he and Eddie looked at each other. Berry was beaming. "I know you've heard about it and have seen the flyers. It's going to be a big, big, show. It's a long way from here, but I think you'll find it's worth the trip."

It suddenly hit Eddie–they were going to be on the same stage with Bill Monroe!

Now, just like with any other banjo player, Earl Scruggs was Eddie's biggest hero. He'd practically invented how to play the banjo, and whenever Scruggs started picking you knew there were going to be fireworks. Eddie loved to watch Flatt & Scruggs play on the Martha White television show and loved to hear them tear into the sponsor's theme song. "You bake right with Martha White," they sang, gathered around the microphone.

Earl was the greatest, but everyone talked about Bill Monroe like he was Moses or something.

"This cakewalk is going to feature The Twelve-Year-Old Terror of the Five String Banjo, Eddie Kane of Sand Mountain, Alabama," Berry continued. Then he turned to Eddie. "Cut loose, Boy."

Eddie started "Redwing" alone and the cakewalkers chased each other from chair to chair. He unexpectedly cut the song on the chorus, and one of the men tumbled to the floor as everyone laughed. The principal quickly pulled out another chair and Eddie resumed playing.

There were 24 cakes given out that night, and Eddie played for every cakewalk. When it was over he wasn't even tired. He hadn't thought about the music at all. It just poured out of him.

And he did feel as if he were indeed the Twelve-Year-Old Terror of the Five String Banjo.

CHAPTER XIII

Dixie Breakdown

Florida!

It was the most exotic place Eddie could imagine. He closed his eyes and pictured palm trees and orange juice and beaches and sand and alligator wrestlers and hula girls.

"Hula girls is in Hawaii!" Cecil admonished him earlier that day in the car when he had been telling Murray everything he wanted to see when they got there.

"They've got mermaids," Murray told him. "Gals who breathe from hoses under the water and do a kind of water ballet."

"Mermaids?" Cecil growled. "You're dreaming!"

"I saw it on a newsreel once. Bathing beauties who breathe from air hoses swim and dance under water. You can sit at this restaurant and watch them through a big window."

That night Eddie worked his way down in the backseat of the car, his banjo still in his lap. They had practiced all the way across lower Alabama. They had to look sharp for Mr. Monroe, Berry kept telling them. Finally his uncle put down his mandolin, folded his jacket for a pillow, and drifted off to sleep.

Eddie fell asleep, too, and was dreaming that the girl at the dry cleaners was swimming in a Florida mermaid show when he heard Murray calling his name.

"Hey! Eddie! You asleep?"

Eddie pushed himself forward and leaned behind Murray, who was at the steering wheel. "What time is it?"

"Around midnight." He passed his transistor radio over his shoulder. "Murray the K's playing a good bluegrass song."

Eddie had heard all sorts of things in the middle of the night listening to that crazy man's radio show. He'd heard Ricky Nelson, the Marvelettes, Elvis, Roy Orbison, Bill Haley and the Comets, Chuck Berry, Jerry Lee Lewis, Ray Charles, and a bunch of others. But he had never heard anything resembling bluegrass. He put the plug in his ear and listened.

"Ah, it's just Elvis doing 'Blue Moon of Kentucky,'" he said, keeping his voice low so he wouldn't wake either of his uncles or Cecil.

"That's right. And do you know who wrote 'Blue Moon of Kentucky?'"

Eddie shrugged.

"Bill Monroe. He had a bluegrass hit with it before Elvis made it rock."

Eddie wasn't sure he liked that. Up on Sand Mountain folks didn't approve of messing with songs. You played a tune like your grandfather played it, and like his father before him. "Do you think that's right, him taking that song like that?"

Murray looked at him and smiled. Eddie thought Murray had something to say about that, but Murray looked at Cecil and kept quiet. Sometimes Cecil pretends to be asleep so he can eavesdrop, Murray had told him.

"I can't believe we're playing a show with Mr. Monroe," Eddie said.

Murray nodded.

"What's it like?"

He had asked Murray this question many times before in the dead of the night as the old car raced through the darkness. Murray had played a show in Ohio when Bill Monroe was the star attraction. He'd seen him in New Jersey, too, out in the country, in a grange hall.

"It's like being in church," Murray said. "His voice is high and lonesome and if you close your eyes you can see the morning mist burning off Jerusalem Ridge."

Eddie knew from a song that Jerusalem Ridge was up on the farm in Kentucky where Bill Monroe grew up.

"Then, WHANG!" Murray continued. "He hits a chord on that old mandolin of his and it's louder than a Baptist piano. It feels like it reverberates here," he said, thumping his chest with an open hand. "Now, don't get me wrong. Your uncle Berry is a good mandolin player. He's one of the best. But he's not Bill Monroe. He didn't invent this music that we're playing."

What if Bill Monroe peers out from under his cowboy hat at me when I'm playing on stage tomorrow? Eddie wondered. I'll probably faint.

Suddenly there was a hiss and the old car shuddered. Steam blew out from under the hood and condensed in droplets on the windshield.

"Uh-oh," Murray said, wrestling the car to the shoulder of the road as Cecil, Berry, and Byron stirred and woke.

"What is it?" Berry said.

"She's running hot. Might be a busted hose."

"Might be." Berry sounded skeptical.

The car had died in the tall weeds on the side of the road. Berry rolled down his window and craned his neck. "Where are we?"

Murray had been driving, but hadn't seen anything but the centerline of the highway for a couple of hours. "Someplace between here and there."

Cecil opened the door and stepped out of the car and looked at his wristwatch. "Somewhere around the panhandle, I reckon." He turned right and then left, as if he could see into the darkness. "It's all colored down here. I don't know who we'll find who knows diddly about cars."

Murray opened the hood and they all leaned over the engine. "Stinks," is all he said.

Byron stuck his hands in his pockets, turned, and started walking up the road.

"Holler if you find anyone," Berry called

after him.

Murray, Eddie, Cecil, and Berry waited silently. It was a moonless night and they could hardly see anything in front of them except occasional flashes of light. Eddie's eyes danced from one golden spark to the next. Fireflies, he thought. He'd see one flash and then he'd try to anticipate where it might reappear. It would be a shame if his uncles didn't get to play with Mr. Monroe. How long could they keep going playing cakewalks and covered dish suppers?

They had waited for more than an hour when they heard a sputtering motor off in the distance. It slowly got louder. Then flickering, yellow headlights appeared and drew closer. An old pick-up truck pulled up beside them. The truck's transmission groaned in protest as the driver worked to get it in reverse. Finally he succeeded and the truck whined as he backed up and made an arc so the truck was in front of the car.

The driver got out and walked toward them. Someone got out on the passenger side, too. The truck was rumbling and coughing and shuddering. Eddie could see the driver was a Negro man in dark coveralls and a ballcap pulled low. Without saying anything he leaned over the side of the pickup, pulled a chain from the bed, and dragged it over the side of the truck. The clanking links snaked behind him as he dropped to his knees, rolled over on his back, and began attaching the chain to the bumper of the car.

It was Byron who had been in the passenger's seat of the truck. "He's got kind of a garage a little ways up the road," he offered.

Cecil leaned forward. All he could see were the man's legs sticking out from under the car. "I don't know about this," he said, stroking his chin. "Isn't there anyone else?"

"Well, why don't you just keep walking, and if you find anyone else out here in the middle of nowhere who can help, just give out a big 'hooty-hoot' and we'll all come running."

Cecil shrugged. "I'm just trying to spare you trouble, that's all."

After the man got the car hitched to the truck they set off for the garage. Cecil, Murray, and Eddie rode in the car. Byron and Berry climbed in the cab of the truck. Murray steered as the two vehicles crept along.

"Watch his tail lights. We don't want to ram him," Cecil instructed. "'Course, I'd be surprised if the taillights worked on that old bucket of bolts."

The man's garage was one of a few buildings that constituted a tiny crossroads community. There was a small church, a crooked cross atop its steeple; a weathered one-story post office with a large picture window; a boarded-up bank; a store with a couple of gas pumps out front; and another building away from the others with yellow light spilling from the windows. A bare bulb dangling in front of the garage was practically the only light in town. Dozens of cars in various states of disrepair were parked in front of the building. Some were on blocks, some were missing hoods or doors or windows. After hopping out of the cab to open the doors of the garage, the driver pulled his truck and the old car into the building.

"The water hose is right there," Cecil said after the hood had been popped and the mechanic began looking over the engine. "Just see if you can patch it up so we can make a run to the nearest town where a real mechanic can look at it."

The mechanic stepped back from the car for a moment and studied Cecil.

Byron shot Cecil a glance and then took a step towards the mechanic. "We'd appreciate anything you could do to help us out," he said, smiling. "We know it's not exactly business hours."

The mechanic took a rag from his pocket, wiped his hands, and leaned over the engine, and studied it for a minute. "That busted hose you got fixed wasn't busted."

Byron and Berry stepped in for a closer look. Cecil leaned against a tool chest and crossed his arms and legs.

"You got a new water hose a while back," he said, pointing at the radiator. "That wasn't your problem. Probably had a bad thermostat. Now you've done ruined your water pump driving it like that."

Eddie remembered the repair Cecil's mechanic had made a while back. He turned to check Murray's reaction but saw that his friend was at the open door, his head thrust outside.

"Hey–"

Murray held up his hands to quiet him. "Listen."

Eddie stood silently. At first he just heard the wind in the trees. Then he heard it, too.

Music.

"It's coming from over there," Murray said, marching toward it without looking back.

"Murray!" Eddie called after him, but Murray kept walking. Eddie looked back in the garage. The men were huddled around the car. The mechanic had leaned over the car and had just about been swallowed up by it. They'd be a while, Eddie decided. "Wait up!" he called to Murray. "I'm coming!"

Eddie hustled to catch up with Murray and spooked a lean dog under a car. The dog loped across the highway. Eddie couldn't see much, but he could hear an occasional rock tumble underfoot on the path as he scrambled after Murray.

They crept around the side of the building, looked in the window, and saw about a dozen people inside. A couple of men were playing pool; two people were sitting at a table, talking. The others danced to the music of a four-piece band.

"Can you make out what they're playing?" Eddie asked.

Murray shook his head. "It ain't 'The Great Speckled Bird.' I guarantee you that."

Eddie put his ear to the window. He could feel the glass vibrate with each thump on the bass. "I don't think I've heard anything like that on Sand Mountain."

"No kidding."

Murray went to the door, but Eddie remained in place.

"Come on," Murray urged.

CHAPTER XIV

We Live in Two Different Worlds

It was smoky and dim inside, and everyone looked at them for a moment as they stood in the door. The dancers stopped swaying and checked them out, but the music kept going, and presently the dancers fell back into the rhythm. Murray and Eddie took a seat at a table near the door.

One of the men was playing the drums. Another musician was blowing a harmonica. Eddie had heard harmonica players before, but none like this fellow. The notes he blew were long and deep and reedy, and he could twist and bend each one of them to make them fit the music. The man on the right was playing an electric bass guitar through an amplifier. It sounded like Cecil's bass fiddle, but it wasn't nearly as big. Sure would be easier to travel with one of them instead of strapping Cecil's big old fiddle to the top of the car, Eddie thought.

The man in the middle was playing an electric guitar, but he wasn't chording it like Byron. It was hard for Eddie to see, but apparently the man was holding a round piece of metal in his left hand and sliding it on the strings. Eddie had seen a fellow play Hawaiian guitar with Roy Acuff once on a television show, and he slid a bar up and down the strings, too. But this was an entirely different sound. It was wild and raw most of the time, but sweet and light sometimes, too.

The song they were playing wasn't fast like one of the breakdowns The Bragger Brothers did, and even though it had a slow, steady beat– boom!boom!boom!–Eddie could feel the bass drum marking time–it had the energy and power of a fast song.

"He's playing slide guitar," Murray said, nodding at the band. "I've never heard one on an electric guitar."

Then the guitarist started singing. And that didn't sound like The Bragger Brothers, either. Just about every one of the songs his uncles sang were real high. In fact, Berry sang what he called "high tenor." But this man's voice was low and rumbled and creaked and he could bend it and twist it to match the notes from the harmonica or the slide guitar. Sometimes it sounded like a cry. Sometimes a shout. It sure fit the music, though.

"He doesn't sound very happy."

Murray smiled and said, "He's fine. He's got

the blues."

At the end of the song the man behind the counter came to Eddie and Murray's table. "What you want?" he asked.

"You have any soda?" Murray asked.

The man's eyes narrowed. "Say what?"

"A Coke or something like that? Or a Nehi?'

The man didn't say anything, but returned to the counter.

"Make it two," Murray called after him, raising his voice to be heard over the band, which started another song.

Eddie drummed his fingers on the table and listened to the man sing about freedom. Eddie couldn't make out all the lyrics, but he understood the point of the song was that the singer wanted to be free of something. Free of this world, or free of a woman, or free from day-to-day troubles. But freedom wasn't coming soon enough or wasn't big enough. He noticed that every now and then people would turn and stare at Murray and him. But it didn't occur to him that they were the only white people in the place until the owner set a grape Nehi in front of him and he saw the dark skin on the back of his hand and the lighter skin on the man's palm. Then one of the women dancing just stared at him. I've done that, Eddie realized. When I got off Sand Mountain and saw Negroes for the first time, I just kept looking at them. Studying them.

I've never been in a place where everyone else didn't look like me or talk like me, he thought. It's a peculiar feeling. Is this what it feels like to be different?

"You ain't from around here, are you?" the man asked after he had set a Coca-Cola in front of Murray.

Oh no, Eddie thought. Here we go again.

Murray took a drink from his bottle and shook his head. "No, we're not."

"Staying or passing through?"

"Passing through."

The man took an empty chair, turned it backward, and sat down at the table with them. "Nobody's never done nothing but passed through." He took a towel that was draped on his shoulder and wiped his hands and then his forehead. "We can't vote, can't get our roads paved, the colored school's about to fall down, they ain't no doctor to get peoples well, and they ain't no jobs. We don't really need people passing through. We need folks who are going to stay here and help change things."

Murray and Eddie didn't know what to say, so they nodded, then listened to the band.

"We're ready for change. Reverend King says it's time for change. But who's gonna do the changing? Nothin's changed in the forty years I've lived here."

The man singing the song was moaning now, and the slide guitar matched him. It was a lonesome sound. It made Eddie think about how far off the mountain he was.

"The N-doubleA-C-P says it wants college kids from up north to come down for the summer and teach school, help us register to vote, build hospitals, things such as that. Something tells me they'll never find us." He pursed his lips and sighed. "Fifty cent."

Murray dug a couple of quarters out of his pocket and handed them over.

"We're musicians," Eddie offered, thinking maybe it excused them from other obligations.

"Musicians?" The man folded his arms. "You the stealing kind?"

Murray blinked. "We just came in to listen for a bit."

"That pretty boy singer—what's his name? Elvis?"

Murray and Eddie nodded.

"Sings that 'Hound Dog.' 'You Aint' Nothin' But a Hound Dog.'"

He stood and turned the chair around.

"Big Momma Thornton sang that on the Chitlin' Circuit for years. Sang it right there one night," he said, nodding at where the band was playing. "That's her song. Ask anyone here. White boy steals it, sings it on Ed Sullivan, and he's sittin' pretty. Big Momma's still singing in joints like this." He turned towards the counter. "I guess they take our music because we don't have anything else worth wanting. We need help, and when people come, they take the only thing we got."

Murray and Eddie sat and listened to the music a while longer until they heard the door open and saw Cecil standing in the doorway. He surveyed the scene and shook his head. He turned around and walked away.

"I think the car's ready," Murray said.

They hustled out and caught up with Cecil.

Raising Kane   109

"God-awfullest noise I've heard in all my put togethers," he said.

Eddie turned to Murray. He smiled, looked down, put his hands in his pockets, and kept walking. "That other town, they were mad at us because they thought we were outsiders trying to cause trouble. Here they're mad at us because we're not."

Eddie thought about that as they walked in the darkness. Sometimes he didn't know what people wanted from him.

"That fool mechanic is pulling a water pump off some other junk heap in his yard that don't run and is putting it on ours," Cecil told them, looking over his shoulder. "He says it'll work, but it's not even the same kind of car. You could have stayed and listened to that noise all night, if you ask me. We ain't going anywhere till we find us a real mechanic."

When they got to the garage all Eddie could see of the tow truck man was his two legs sticking out from under the car, just like when they had left. Byron and Berry were leaning against the workbench.

"I got 'em," Cecil said, "but I don't think we're going anywhere for a long time."

"Hush, Cecil," Byron said. "He's just about finished."

Eddie looked at the cluttered workbench. It reminded him of the one in the garage at Doyle's Gas Station back home. There were fan belts hanging from a pegboard and black, greasy bolts scattered on the tabletop. There was a long row of jelly jars at the back of the bench filled with nuts and bolts and washers and cotter pins. There were grease guns, screwdrivers, wrenches, hammers, quarts of oil and transmission fluid, and a big can of Pink Goo hand-cleaning compound.

The mechanic slid out from under the car, wiped his hands on a rag, and motioned for Byron to start the engine.

Byron got behind the wheel and the engine started up right away. Byron and Berry looked at each other and smiled. Eddie and Murray started to get in the car.

"Just a minute," Cecil said, turning and facing the mechanic. "We better let it run a bit and see if it's gonna run hot."

They stayed where they were, not saying a word, not moving. Byron kept his eye on the temperature gauge. Ever so often he'd give a report. "Looks good."

A few minutes later: "Still looks good."

And finally, after nearly ten minutes: "She's running cooler than she has for days," he said, smiling.

Cecil crossed his arms and narrowed his eyes. "Where'd a fellow like you learn about cars?" he asked the mechanic.

"Army."

"European or Pacific Theater?"

The mechanic leaned down and pulled the dipstick out of the old car and checked the oil level. "I was in France and Belgium and Germany."

Berry snapped his fingers. "Red Ball Express," he said, pointing an accusing finger at the mechanic.

The man said nothing. He replaced the dipstick and then pulled out a screwdriver to make a minute adjustment on the carburetor.

"They kept those trucks rolling twenty-four hours a day," Berry said, turning to the others. "More than once we were stranded, in front of the column, out of gas." He turned back to the mechanic. "I was in the Third Armored under Patton," he said. Then he turned again to Cecil and Berry. "It was a beautiful sight to see those trucks with the red ball painted on the door roll up and unload. That meant we could get going. We weren't sitting ducks anymore."

The mechanic unscrewed the caps on the battery and inserted his little finger in each cell to check the fluid. "They didn't think us colored boys could fight," he said. "Wouldn't give us the chance. I spent most of my time in the army at first digging graves. Then when they had to move all those supplies to keep the tanks running they took all us noncombatants and put us in the trucks. Most of us in the Express was Negro boys."

He stepped back from the car and put his hands on his hips to give the engine a final inspection. "I drove and repaired beat up-trucks, machine-gunned trucks, trucks that had rolled over land mines, trucks that had turned over in ditches. I got strafed by German planes and drove into an ambush where three of my buddies were killed. But we kept rolling." He slammed the hood of the car. "I think you and your water pump are going to be just fine."

Byron got out from behind the wheel to pay

the man. Everyone else got in the car.

"That's that," Byron said when he got back in. He put the car in gear and he waved to the mechanic as they turned on to the highway.

Byron looked in the rearview mirror and found Eddie. "Whatever you do, don't tell your mother you spent the night in a roadhouse."

"Yes, sir," he replied, not sure what a roadhouse was.

They rode in silence for a while. Murray gave Eddie his radio and he turned the dial, looking for baseball scores. He heard Murray the K say it was two in the morning.

Berry stretched his arms in the front seat. Eddie was sitting between Cecil and Murray in the back. Cecil sat quietly, his arms folded.

"I read once Eisenhower said we couldn't have won the war without the Red Ball Express," Berry said to no one in particular.

They sat in silence for several miles and through a couple of tiny towns. Eddie had just about fallen asleep when Murray turned to Cecil. "Hey," he said.

"Hey what?"

"Did you get your bass fiddle?"

CHAPTER XV

Heavy Traffic Ahead

"I wish we could make a little detour to see the ocean," Byron said when Eddie stirred the next morning. Eddie's neck was stiff and his back ached from sitting up and sleeping in the car. He squinted and blinked, trying to adjust to the daylight. "You've never seen the ocean, have you?"

"No, sir," Eddie replied, his mouth dry. He shielded his eyes with a hand. It sure was bright. He looked outside and saw a brilliant sun shining on a flat land with palm trees lining the road and white sandy soil covered with scrub pine.

"Florida," Murray announced, anticipating Eddie's question. He nodded at rows of trees in sprawling fields. "See the orange groves?"

Eddie nodded.

Murray stuck his head out the window and then pulled it back in. "Smell 'em."

Eddie took a deep breath. It reminded him of Christmas because there was always an orange in the toe of the sock he hung on the mantle. "Is this Miami?" he asked.

Cecil snorted. "That's 'way to the south. We're headed for Middleburg." He checked his wristwatch. "We gonna make it?" he asked Byron, who was still driving.

"We'll make it," he said, staring straight ahead. Eddie wondered who he was trying to convince.

Cecil raised his hand to his mouth and chewed on a stubborn hangnail. "Mr. Monroe's not going to like it if we're late," he said.

"He said we'll make it," Berry repeated slowly. He was leaning back in his seat with his eyes shut.

"They say Mr. Monroe's traveling again like the old days," Cecil said, turning to Murray because he seemed to be the only one who would listen. "I saw him back in '40 in Newton, North Carolina. He had a big tent–bigger than the biggest revival preacher ever dreamed of having– and he was selling programs and photographs and souvenir books and I don't know what all. There was a searchlight on the back of an old truck that lit up the sky and I remember watching the nighthawks swarm and circle in the light as it slowly went back and forth. He had a bunch of opening acts–there was a cowboy singer and a pretty gal who sang and played the accordion. There was a clown who had a pet monkey on his shoulder who wandered the crowd, giving the kids penny candy.

"And then Bill and Charlie came out on stage." He elbowed Eddie and offered an explanation. "Charlie was his brother he used to play with but they had a falling out not too long after that. Anyway, they come out and they're wearing these puffed-out horse riding pants and long, long, black leather boots. I mean, they really looked like some dandy Kentucky Colonels. And I'm telling you, everyone went wild when they started singing and playing. And the people—you can't believe the kind of crowds he was drawing back then. There were cars as far as you could see. Some folks came by wagon, and you could hear the mules braying in the distance when he did 'Muleskinner Blues.'"

Cecil put his hands behind his head and sat back in his seat like he was settling in for a nap after a big meal. "Wouldn't it be something if things were like that again?"

Eddie thought of shows The Bragger Brothers had played since he'd gone on the road with them. PTA cakewalks. Automobile dealership sales. Potluck dinners at sour smelling VFW posts. Daybreak shows at tiny radio stations in the middle of dusty cotton fields. Yes, it would really be something if things were like they were when Bill Monroe had his tent show.

"Mr. Monroe wouldn't take kindly to it if we were late. That's all I'm saying," Cecil concluded.

Eddie's stomach grumbled, but he knew they wouldn't be stopping for breakfast today. Maybe not even lunch. He wasn't sure, but judging by the way Byron was driving, it was still a long way to Middleburg.

They were racing the clock, but finally about mid-day Eddie could tell from the expression on his Uncle Byron's face that they were going to make it. Berry's spirits were buoyed, too, and he made Eddie and Murray pick up their instruments so they could practice. "Fireball Mail," he said, and so Eddie kicked it off as they raced through the instrumental. Murray slipped out his pocketknife and used it for a slide on his violin like the blues guitar player had done the night before. It sounded weird–kind of like a kid tuning a plastic dime store guitar–and Eddie thought Cecil would complain about the new, strange sound. Before he could say anything, though, Byron slowed the car.

"Look at this," he said.

The road was choked with automobiles. People had parked helter-skelter on the side of the road, in ditches, in fields, in yards, and in driveways. Everywhere they looked they saw people carrying lawn chairs and picnic coolers and blankets.

"You reckon this is all for Mr. Monroe?" Cecil asked, but no one said anything. Eddie hadn't ever seen this many people in one place, not even at the county fair.

They crept along with the rest of the traffic until a highway patrolman at an intersection stopped them. "You playing here?" he asked, eyeing Cecil's bass fiddle on the top of the car.

"If this is the Bill Monroe show we are," Byron said. "It looks more like an Elvis crowd."

"There's a lot of folks here, that's for sure," the officer agreed. He motioned for one of his colleagues to drag a barricade out of the way. "Let 'em through," he shouted. Then he leaned back to Byron. "You better get going. I think they're about to get started."

They were directed to a parking area behind a temporary stage that had been assembled by parking two flatbed trailers next to each other. A man in overalls and a straw cowboy hat ran cables to the microphones that were set up, and lights were trained on the stage for an evening performance. There was only one thing missing: the people.

Eddie distributed the hats from behind the front seat, and they got out of the car. "Where is everyone?" Murray asked.

And then a tall man in a white shirt, black pants, skinny black tie, and big white Stetson hat appeared from behind a bus. He was carrying a beat-up mandolin. "They're at the ball field," he said.

"Howdy, Bill," Byron said, offering his hand. "It's been a while."

"That it has, Byron Bragger, that it has," said Bill Monroe.

Eddie couldn't believe it. Maybe Elvis was big on the radio, but there was no one more popular on Sand Mountain than Bill Monroe. When a Bill Monroe song came on the radio at Doyle's Gas Station, the talk stopped and everyone just listened. If Mr. Doyle were fixing a flat he'd stop worrying with the lug nuts and sit back on his haunches and rock to the music.

Byron, Berry, and Cecil made small talk with Monroe while Eddie and Murray quietly stood beside the car.

"Looks like it's going to be a big show tonight," Murray said.

"Yep."

"You nervous?"

"Not yet."

"Hey!" Byron called, motioning them over. "This is Mr. Monroe," he said, once they joined the others. "And Bill, this is Murray Singer, our fiddler, and this here is my nephew, Eddie Kane."

Monroe peered down his nose at Eddie. "The Twelve-Year-Old Terror of the Five String Banjo."

Eddie blushed.

Monroe laughed. "I heard you on the radio. You're a crackerjack banjo player. What I want to know, though, is do you play any baseball?"

The question took Eddie by surprise. "Yes sir. A little. I was going to play at Fort Payne this summer but . . . but I'm pickin' instead."

"How 'bout you, son. You ever play ball?"

Murray smiled. "I was on the championship stickball team at P.S. 132 in the third grade."

"Well, here's the thing," Monroe said, thrusting his hands in his pockets. "Some of the local boys have challenged my boys to a game."

"Just like the old days," Cecil piped in,

rubbing his hands.

"Yes sir. We've been doing a bit of this as we've been touring this summer. But I'm a couple of players short. I got uniforms that would fit you two if you're willing."

Cecil's smile faded. "Them?"

Monroe turned and looked at him over the top of his glasses.

"I mean, they're nice kids, but, well, the one's just a boy, and the other—well, he's a New York Jew."

Murray put his hands on his hips. "What's that supposed to mean?"

"Now, I didn't mean anything by it, Murray," Cecil said, shaking his head. "But your kind ain't exactly known for ball playin'."

"You ever hear of Hank Greenberg? Or how about Sandy Koufax? And Norm and Larry Sherry?"

Eddie knew Sandy Koufax was just about the best pitcher in the major leagues. But he didn't know he was Jewish.

Berry put an arm around Cecil and then playfully knocked his hat down over his eyes. "Don't take it so hard. Bill can't use you. You're too old and too fat to be running the bases."

Everyone but Cecil laughed, and Monroe took out a big handkerchief and blew his nose. "I don't care what you are," he said, looking at Murray. "I know you're a good fiddler. If you're a ball player, I can use you." Then he turned to Eddie. "You, too."

Eddie held up a red stirrup sock and admired the way it looked against the gray jersey, which had red piping around the collar and down the front. "These look like big league uniforms," he said.

Murray nodded. He turned over his jersey and read the letters across the back. "Bill's Boys." He rubbed the material between his fingers. "Wool. I bet these things are twenty years old."

"From back in the days when Bill had the big tent show?"

Murray nodded.

Eddie and Murray hurriedly dressed in a four-seater outhouse just behind the bleachers at the ballfield in the park. All day long, they had been told, people from all over the county had been gathering for the big game and the show that would follow that evening. Eddie didn't know what was more exciting–and unnerving–playing on Mr. Monroe's team or appearing on the same stage with him. "Murray, what's stickball?"

"It's what you play when you live in the city and you don't have a field or a park for a game. You got a manhole for home, a storm drain for first, another manhole for second, and a mailbox for third."

"And you were on a championship team?"

"Well, we were winning until Mr. Fabrizio started working on his Hudson and spread the front end all over left field."

Eddie tugged the laces on his right shoe and tied them. In the background he could hear the crowd that was gathering in the bleachers. "I don't think you're going to have to worry about Mr. Fabrizio and his Hudson here."

CHAPTER XVI

The Red-Haired Boy

Eddie Kane had every excuse for playing a lousy game that afternoon. He'd never played on a real team, he hadn't swung a bat in weeks, and playing in front of a park full of yelling fans was a lot different than catching a ball when it rolled off the roof in your backyard. And while he was in good banjo-playing shape–the fingers on his left hand were tough and callused, and he could stand for hours now with his banjo and not get tired–he wasn't in very good shape to be hitting or fielding. Still, when he tugged the bill of his cap and pulled it low to keep the searing sun out of his eyes and dug in the dirt with the toe of his sneaker and saw the brown dust swirl, he was thrilled. It could have been the All-Star game or the World Series, as far as he was concerned.

Mr. Monroe started him at second base, but he missed a couple of hot grounders. Eddie was mortified. It was the same feeling he used to get when he messed up a banjo solo with everyone watching. Monroe didn't say anything to him in the dugout, but moved him to right field in the third inning. There wasn't much action there. He cleanly fielded a couple of grounders that got past the first baseman, but the Middleburg Titans got the lead when he lost a pop fly in the sun and dropped it.

"It's gonna be all right now," Mr. Monroe said when Eddie trotted into the dugout at the end of the inning, fighting tears. "We're still in this thing."

Which was true, thanks to the bass player in Bill's band. He was a small guy–so small it was hard to imagine him reaching up the neck and playing a bull fiddle–but he had hit two home runs in three trips to the plate.

"Did you ever notice in a lot of bands the smallest guy plays the biggest instrument?" Murray called over his shoulder to Eddie. Murray was on deck and was swinging two bats to get loosened up. He'd had a pretty good game so far. He got on base a couple of times and was knocked in once by the bass player. And he hadn't embarrassed himself in left field.

Eddie struck out every time he was at the plate. The ball was zooming in at him. He couldn't even see it.

"Kid, he's about twice your age," Murray said, pointing to the other team's pitcher on the mound. "He's getting the best of just about all of us."

Monroe didn't suit up. He was pacing in the dugout, and sometimes after someone on his team struck out or dropped a ball he would take off his ballcap and slap it against the bench or the fence. He's excitable, like Uncle Berry, Eddie thought.

"Look at those thick glasses of his," Murray whispered to Eddie on the bench. "I heard that he's got terrible eyesight. Lots of times people think he's ignoring them because he's a snob, but really, he can't see them until he gets real close to them."

By the seventh inning Eddie was praying that no more balls would come to him in right field. I just don't want to mess up anymore, he thought. In fact, he had to field a couple more slow grounders, which he did without any trouble.

There was plenty of trouble elsewhere, though. Monroe's pitcher got wild and walked in a run. Then he hit the next batter and the benches cleared and everyone crowded around the mound, looking for a fight. Eddie thought maybe he should join them, but when he glanced over to the stands he saw Byron and Berry motioning him to stay put. Murray sauntered up the mound but stayed well out of harm's way. The fans were hooting and hollering, but Mr. Monroe cooled everyone down and the game resumed.

Then the pitcher walked in another run and Bill's Boys were down by two. Monroe pulled the pitcher and sent in Chubby, his fiddle player, to throw.

"Hoo boy," the centerfielder called over to

Murray while the new pitcher took his warm-up tosses. "Chubby throws junk. When he's on, he's on. But when he's not, they hit the daylights out of it."

During a Saturday Game of the Week last year Eddie's father had explained to him what it meant for a pitcher to throw junk. "They don't throw fast, because they don't have any power. Usually it's an old pitcher who's blown out his arm. They throw knuckleballs, screwballs, stuff like that. If the wind's right and the humidity's right the ball will dance all over the plate like a butterfly. It drives batters crazy."

Eddie figured Chubby must have worn out his arm sawing on the fiddle.

"If the weather's not right, though," his father had continued, "or if he doesn't have his touch or luck's not with him, they'll hit the cover off everything thrown by a junker."

But that inning Chubby's junk was working, and he retired the side without any more runs scoring. Some of the players on the other team yelled that he was throwing spitballs or putting greasy kid stuff from his hair on the ball, and the ump called for the ball and carefully inspected it, rolling it over and over in his hands. He couldn't find anything.

And so Bill's Boys went into the top of the ninth inning down by two runs. They got a small rally going and got a couple of men on base, but then their luck ran out. The Middleburg pitcher got his stuff back.

Eddie checked the lineup. It would be nice if

they won, but frankly, he just hoped the whole thing ended before he got up to bat again. He didn't want to be the goat, the last out. What was I thinking when I daydreamed about playing ball and scoring all those runs? he wondered.

The next two batters struck out, and then Mr. Monroe called Eddie's name. Eddie realized what had happened. By bringing Chubby into the game, Mr. Monroe had exhausted his bench. There was no one left to bat for Eddie. And he hadn't got a hit all day.

"It's all right, Son," Mr. Monroe said, putting his hand on Eddie's shoulder as he walked to the plate. Eddie could tell by the sound of his voice that he was already conceding defeat. "Do your best."

Murray had some practical advice for him, though. "Listen. It's just like music. You're trying too hard, you're thinking too hard about where the ball is going to be. When it feels right, just stick the bat out there. You don't have to swing hard. It'll be all right."

Two outs, men on first and second. If he struck out the game was over.

Eddie swung hard at the first pitch and didn't come close.

"Take it easy," Murray called from the bench. "You don't have to kill it. Trust your instincts."

Still, Eddie couldn't help but swing with all his might at the next pitch. He missed and stumbled in the dirt. Some in the crowd laughed. Two pitches, two strikes.

"Just stick the bat where you think he's liable to put it," Murray urged.

Eddie was so sure it would be the last pitch of the game that he couldn't bear to watch. So he closed his eyes and just held the bat over the plate.

Zing!

Eddie heard a tiny noise and felt his hands shake. Then there was a gigantic sound as the fans erupted, cheering and yelling. He opened his eyes and saw the ball lazily rolling along the line toward third base. The pitcher had accidentally hit his bat with the ball. It was a glancing blow, but it was a perfect bunt.

He tore off for first base with all his might. The catcher's legs were just about asleep from squatting so long and he stumbled as he picked up the ball. He tried to get the lead runner instead of the easy out at first. The ball sailed over the third baseman's head. One run in!

The left fielder chased the ball as the second of Bill's Boys rounded third. The throw missed the cutoff man and again the catcher stumbled as he went to his right for the ball. Another run in!

Eddie's legs and arms were churning as fast as they could go as he rounded third. The only thing he could see was Murray, who had jumped off the bench and was running alongside him, windmilling his arm, a signal to Eddie that he should keep running. "Go! Go! Go!" he screamed.

Eddie could see the pitcher was racing to home plate, too. He was going to take the throw from the catcher and try to make the out. Eddie just kept running, then he threw his feet out in front of him to slide, threw his hands above his head, and closed his eyes.

When he opened them all he could see was a big cloud of dust and the pitcher holding the ball in his glove, showing it to the umpire.

"Safe! You missed the tag!"

And now there was more commotion on the field than when the pitcher had hit that batter. Everyone on Mr. Monroe's team was dancing and shouting and waving. The little bass player picked up Eddie and carried him off the field. Some of the fans were stomping and screaming. Once Eddie was set down Murray hugged him and Mr. Monroe shook his hand. "If you play that banjo like you swing that bat, I want you in my band," he said. Then the old man leaned against the fence, folded his arms, and settled in to watch the end of the game.

Brent Davis

CHAPTER XVII

Bright Morning Stars

Chubby's junk held, and Bill's Boys won the game.

Eddie was exhausted after the baseball game—mainly from all the excitement—and he fell asleep in the back of the car after changing into his street clothes in the big outhouse. At dusk he stirred, rolled his neck and shoulders to encourage a little circulation, and looked out the window and saw everyone gathering for the concert: families with picnic baskets carried by the mothers and folded lawn chairs under the arms of the fathers. Men with their hands folded behind the bib of their overalls as they made their way along the sandy path. Children playing tag, racing after one another, looking back occasionally to make sure they weren't too far ahead of their parents. There were young kids, too, about Murray's age, some in sunglasses, a few in beards, carrying blankets and coolers. College kids, Eddie guessed, and he realized it was the first time he'd seen them at one of the shows. As he watched the people streaming through the woods he realized this would be the largest crowd The Bragger Brothers had played before all summer. He thought back to the first show he'd played with his uncles and remembered how nervous he'd been that time at the fish fry. Then he remembered playing at the VFW after that awful day in Montgomery. He could still clearly see the face of the laughing woman and of the man with the baseball bat. But after that day he'd never again imagined them in the audience.

Who all would be in the crowd that night? Would he look out and see a face that would make him freeze? Then he realized it didn't matter. He was a different person now than that scaredy cat who left Sand Mountain the beginning of the summer.

Then he thought of Bill Monroe with that big cowboy hat pulled low and his mandolin cinched up high under his neck, chopping on it like he was taking an axe to a tree. Eddie was going to be playing in front of the man who had more or less invented the music his uncles and everyone else played. And he had to admit that made him nervous.

The show started that night with a local act, a family band in string ties and denim and calico. The smallest of them, a boy who couldn't be more than six or seven, played a guitar so big that it nearly hid him. A girl a little younger than Eddie played the fiddle so hard that hairs broke off the bow with each stroke and whipped in the air around her. Eddie was relieved to see the mother played claw-hammer banjo, strumming with her thumb and finger instead of picking like he did. It was such a different style that no one would compare his playing to hers.

Toward the end of their set everyone but the mother stopped playing their instruments and began a furious dance as she kept hammering on the banjo. There weren't enough of them for an honest-to-goodness square-dance, but they lifted their legs so high and so fast it sounded like an army was marching in on the concert. Eddie rolled his eyes, thinking it was silly for them all to break out in a dance like that, but then he saw Mr. Monroe moving in with them from the wings, dancing a jig and then doing a do-si-do with the youngest girl. The crowd went crazy and Eddie found himself clapping to the beat just like everyone else.

Next up was a brother act, and when Eddie saw the two fellows stand at the single microphone in the middle of the stage with nothing more than a guitar and a mandolin—not even a bass fiddle to lend a little bottom to their sound—he thought this act would fall flat, especially after all the commotion of that family band. However, from the very first song the Whitman Brothers held the crowd spellbound. Their voices were perfectly suited to each other and their "livin' and losin'" songs, as they referred to them in an introduction, drew loud cheers, whistles, and a few "amens" during the applause.

And then The Bragger Brothers took the stage and played the best set of music of the entire summer that Eddie spent with them. He was indeed the Twelve-Year-Old Terror of the Five String Banjo that night, and when the crowd realized he was the kid who had won the ball game that afternoon, they got on their feet and cheered for what seemed forever. Eddie didn't have to think of a single song or lick or note: it all just automatically poured out of his hands. He saw things differently that night. Sometimes it seemed as if he were in the crowd, watching himself play. As the sky went from blue to black and the white stars began popping out he felt as if he were in the heavens, too, looking down at this gathering of people who had come together only because of the music. White and black, he thought, looking into the sky, his fingers ablaze and in motion without him having to think about it. Opposites and yet perfect together.

Then he began to hear things differently that night, too. No matter what the tempo of the song, he could slow it down or speed it up in his mind without ever changing the speed of his fingers. Even though the notes from his banjo were coming out in the usual flurry on "Katy Hill," in his mind he could put whole seasons between them. He could picture spring wildflowers emerging from the wet, dark dirt of Sand Mountain. Then the deep green of summer, the brilliant colors of fall, and then a sprinkling of snow. All of this between two notes.

And he heard a voice, too, in his banjo-playing. A persistent voice he couldn't place. He'd heard voices in his playing before–the sharp crack of a revival preacher's admonitions; the plain, simple, pure tones of the neighbor girl singing softly as she walked to the school bus; the eerie, powerful chords of sacred harp singers at an all-day meeting. He gazed at the black night sky and finally the new voice became clear: it was that singer he'd heard with Murray in the Alabama roadhouse. Whenever Eddie would choke his third string, bending it for bluesy effect, or slide from the second to the third fret, he could hear that blues singer and his reedy harmonica and slide guitar, bending and twisting notes. Eddie looked down at his right and then left hand. It's all in there, he thought. It's all there.

The Bragger Brothers ended their set with two encores, and when it was over Eddie couldn't figure out if they had been playing a long time or if it had happened in a flash.

But Bill Monroe was who everyone came to see, and he did not disappoint. At the end of the concert he called Eddie out on stage to play "Wheel Hoss" with him and his band, and the crowd went crazy again. Eddie took two breaks.

Eddie looked out from under his white Stetson hat as the people cheered and stomped and whistled. His thoughts were elsewhere, though. He pictured his mother at home, looking out over the mountain, a cup of sassafras tea in her hands. She was right. There's something

Raising Kane   133

powerful in this music. And you'd better be careful what you do with it.

Eddie was on the road for only a couple more weeks, and then it was back to Sand Mountain and his chores and school. That summer people all over the Southeast had cheered for him and The Bragger Brothers in show after show. They had driven from one state to the next, from concert to radio show to every event imaginable. But Eddie never got a bigger thrill than the day he played baseball and the banjo with Bill Monroe.

EPILOGUE

Though The Bragger Brothers had a loyal following, they never had a hit record. "If it hadn't been for rock 'n roll–" Berry said to Eddie once, and then he stopped in mid-sentence. "If 'ifs' and 'buts' were candy and nuts we'd all have a very merry Christmas," he finished, shaking his head. The Bragger Brothers kept playing small shows throughout the South and logged hundreds of thousands of miles in a succession of old cars until they were well into their seventies. Byron died of a heart attack working in his garden at his home. Berry's in a VA hospital, where every now and then he plays his mandolin for some of the guys in his ward.

Cecil Reddick got tired of the road and quit the music business after a while and got a job repairing pin setting machines at bowling alleys. But that kept him on the road as much as being in a band, which his wife hated. So he started selling Jewel T products. He would call The Bragger Brothers every now and then, trying to convince them to buy window cleaner or quart bottles of vanilla extract. Finally Byron told him he didn't want any of that junk and not to call anymore.

Murray Singer is a folklorist at the Smithsonian. He still plays music at clubs and parties and festivals. He returned to the South for Freedom Summer, in 1964, when he was a college student, and worked registering black voters in rural Alabama. He made a point of going to the roadhouse where the band had broken down that night and took a carload of people to the courthouse so they could get on the voter rolls.

When Eddie Kane turned 18 he was invited to tour with Bill Monroe and the Bluegrass Boys, but he was in a band with a bunch of other young guys at the time and they were convinced they were going to hit it big. It never happened. He drifted in and out of a half a dozen bands and appeared on the Grand Old Opry many times. No matter where he played–and he went to Japan, among other places, where bluegrass music has a lot of devoted fans–he never felt like he'd left Sand Mountain. I'm carrying it with me, he realized, because its music is in me through and through.

But finally it wasn't enough just to be carrying a part of it with him. So one night after a particularly good show at the Opry, he said, "That's it, boys. I'm going back to Sand Mountain." And for the most part he's been there ever since.

A lot of the old timers who heard him at fish fries and in Odd Fellows halls and at twenty-minute shows between double features at local drive-ins insist Eddie Kane was one of the best to ever pick up the five string. They mention him in the same breath with Earl Scruggs and J.D. Crowe and Don Reno. But Eddie's content today to putter around the farm on the old tractor. He's not played in a club or at a concert in years. They say he jams every now and then with friends.

But if you want to hear him—if you want to learn about the sound that made him the Twelve-Year-Old Terror of the Five-String Banjo—you'd better make a trip to Sand Mountain and hide behind a tree. Because every now and then he likes to walk the old hills and play "Bill Cheatham" or "Soldier's Joy" on that cigar box banjo that still hangs on the wall.

A native of Springfield, Missouri, **Brent Davis** was a television reporter in Savannah, Georgia; taught and produced documentaries in Tuscaloosa, Alabama; and now works for WOSU Public Media in Columbus, Ohio. Saturdays he can often be found at the jam session at Bluegrass Musician's Supply on High Street. He is also the author of *The Spelling Bee*. He has a wife and a son. They have a Corgi and a cat.